Psiscouts #2:

Bright Promise

Don Sakers &
Phil Meade

PSI SCOUTS #2: BRIGHT PROMISE
copyright © 2014, Speed-of-C Productions

This is a work of fiction. All the characters and events portrayed in this book are fictitious, and any resemblance to real people or events is purely coincidental.

Published by
Speed-of-C Productions
811 Camp Meade Rd
Linthicum, MD 21090-3030

ISBN: 978-1-9347-5412-2
First print edition August 2019

Dedicated to:

Priscilla Olson, Brenda Clough,
Jim Gale, Mercy VanVlack, Pam Fremon,
Dan "Renfield" Corcoran,
and Stan Thompson, wherever he is.

Part One:

The Case of the
Living Legends

ROLL CALL:
   Bolt
   Colossus
   Coloumb
   Fade
   Legion
   Mentaxa
   Mimic

INTRODUCING:
   BioLogic 17
   Do-San
   Power Lad
   Power Maid

May AD 2574

EARTHNET alt.trends.commentary on Mon May 9, 2574 Sec: 1
Conf: 1
{RTC RECEIVE ONLY}
[RUNNING ARCHIVE TO Sec:1 Thread: 346] **RESPOND ON Sec:
1 Conf: 2**
FROM: NETJAY [Jav Man] AT 14:02:34

[THIS IS A REALTIME REPORT]

Friends and neighbors, droogs and drooglets, welcome to Scouts'
Island—that's Bedloe's Island, for the woefully uninformed among
you [KEY 977 for background SCOUTS' ISLAND]—for the first-ever
PsiScouts tryouts.

We're standing on the front steps of Scouts Headquarters, and as
we pan over the throng of anxious teeners, there's one question
uppermost in your mind: Which of these lucky kids will have the right
stuff to become a PsiScout?

The competition has been fierce, with applicants lining up since
yesterday morning just for a chance at a tryout. [KEY 324 for
interviews with waiting applicants] Fade, Colossus, and Bolt have
been up since sunrise, talking to the more than three hundred
hopefuls—just a few minutes ago, Bolt told us that her team has now
eliminated all applicants without demonstrated psi abilities, those
who are too old or too young, and even a few of what Bolt called
"weirdos." [KEY 003 for interview with Bolt].

Whether they become Scouts or not, all of today's applicants will
walk away winners. Those without psi abilities are being recruited for
membership in the Youth Corps Rangers, a devoted force already
several thousand strong throughout the Myriad Worlds. Kiddos can
become Irregulars, a branch of the Youth Corps supervised by
PsiScout Legion himself.

The psi-talented teeners who aren't quite ready to be Scouts will
become PsiCadets, to receive training and guidance from all the
Scouts.

Looks like the festivities are about to begin, so we take you now
to PsiScouts' Plaza.

Coulomb, a black-haired teener in maroon and grey accented with red stripes, looked out at the sea of teeners who surrounded PsiScouts Headquarters and whistled. "I had no idea there'd be so many."

Mentaxa, thin, pale of skin and dark of hair, shivered. "They all want to be Scouts. And not one in a hundred has the ability." Her psi talent was telepathy.

De' Colleen Artveldt, the rich old woman who bankrolled the Scouts, laughed. "Looking at you young ones, I'd say it's closer to one in a million." Her face became momentarily serious. "Those who don't qualify as Scouts can join the Rangers. You need dependable, talented people behind the scenes. And you need to make it clear that your values aren't just for those with psi talents. They're for everyone."

Legion, wearing his usual good-natured smile, took a last swig from a juice bulb, then threw the empty bulb smartly into the trash orifice. "My Irregulars know that. They're good kids."

Mentaxa frowned. "That's because they have six of you in charge." Legion could manifest up to six duplicates of himself.

"Mentaxa is right," Mimic said. The shapechanger wore his natural form: he was short, uniformly grey, with large ears, enormous eyes, and a great snout-like nose. His legs were thick and solid, and he had a stubby tail. "The Irregulars are afraid to act up because they never know when Legion is watching."

"Hey, those kids don't behave because they're afraid." Legion sounded hurt. "They behave because they want to."

Fade, a dark-haired, vaguely oriental teener whose talent allowed her to become invisible and move through solid matter, poked her head through the closed door. "Got 'em warmed up," she said. "Now showtime."

"Wait a minute. How many candidates are trying out?"

"Fifteen," Fade answered. "When Colossus gave 'em spiel about how dangerous it be, and Bolt talked about commitment they'd be making, half of 'em turned tail. Come on while these still left."

De' Artveldt held back, forcing the PsiScouts to go before her. Following Legion and Mimic, Coulomb stepped out into the bright sun and total pandemonium. PsiScouts Headquarters, the once-abandoned Statue of Liberty, towered above them.

Two thousand teeners, Coulomb discovered, made more noise than an entire stadium of ironball fans. They were everywhere; if he and the other Scouts had not been on a raised platform, they would be invisible. Out of the corner of his eye Coulomb caught a flock of camera drones, with Jav's no doubt among them, relaying the proceedings to everyone who couldn't crowd into the plaza in person.

Bolt, a gangly red-haired girl in a PsiScouts uniform of two-toned emerald, raised her hands and sent lighting toward the sky. That got their attention. Then, amplifiers maxed out, Bolt cried out, "Are you ready to start?"

"READY!" The sound nearly made Liberty herself quiver.

De' Artveldt stepped forward, standing tall and broad, with an arm about both Bolt and Coulomb and a breeze stirring her silver hair. The crowd fell silent, and stayed that way while Colleen spoke about courage, dedication, and the pride she had in the PsiScouts. By the time she finished, Coulomb was blushing.

Bolt reclaimed center stage, introduced the other six Scouts, then called for the first candidate.

The boy who leapt onto the platform was tall and slim, with shoulder-length dirty blond hair and eyes of deep blue. Wisps of adolescent fuzz clung to his chin. His shapeless green-and-blue shirt was ripped, his black trousers tattered. A massive pair of bright green shoes adorned his feet.

"Tell us your name," Bolt invited.

"I'm Ber Nanda," he replied. He wore no amplifier, but Coulomb's ability to manipulate magnetic fields allowed him to direct the automatic system toward the boy with a nod of his head.

Thrusting out his chin, Nanda said, "As a PsiScout, I take the name Tempest."

Tem-PEST is more like it, Mentaxa thoughtcast. From the hastily-suppressed smiles, Coulomb saw that the others had picked up her comment as well.

"Okay, Tempest," Bolt said. "Why don't you tell us what you can do, and then give a demonstration?"

The newcomer closed his eyes, breathed deeply. Moving with the controlled tension of a martial artist, he spun, gestured, then froze with his right arm extended, pointing across the plaza to where the blue-and-gold banner of the PsiScouts flew just below the flag of the Myriad Worlds.

For a few long seconds, nothing happened. Then, just as the crowd was starting to get restless, both flags stirred. Tempest held his pose, and the breeze became a wind, then a gale. The flags flapped violently, the trees lining the plaza bent, whitecaps showed on the water beyond.

The crowd broke into frenzied applause, Legion clapped the newcomer on the back—and still the gale continued, rising in force. Still Tempest remained frozen in place, pointing.

In a matter of seconds, a triumph became a laughing matter, as nervous twitters spread through the crowd. Those in the path of the wind, however, didn't laugh for long. Teeners scrambled to get out of the gale, laughter turned to screams, and suddenly a disaster was brewing in PsiScouts' Plaza.

Legion hesitantly tapped Tempest on the shoulder. The boy didn't respond. "I...uh, I think you'd better stop."

With an agonized frown, Tempest grunted, "...can't."

Coulomb heard his communit click onto the Scouts' private channel. Bolt said, "All right, we have a dangerous situation. Who has any ideas?"

"I can lift him above the crowd," Colossus volunteered.

"Too risky. Mentaxa?"

Mentaxa already had her eyes closed. "I'm scanning him."

One of the trees tilted, and with a powerful snap a huge limb crashed down in a shower of leaves. It landed with a splash in the water.

"Bolt, this is getting serious. In another second or two we're going to have injuries."

Bolt snapped out orders. "Colossus, get large. Watch where you put your feet, and try to block the wind."

Mentaxa muttered, "He's in a theta-state fugue. Give me a few more seconds and I can—"

"We ain't got seconds," Fade said.

Colossus, twenty meters tall and still growing, stepped gingerly in front of Tempest, bracing himself against the gale.

"If he loses his balance, he'll crush the kids."

Coulomb clenched his fist. saw Legion do the same. He didn't want to hurt Tempest, but if it was the only way—

Tempest shuddered, then pitched forward. Legion and Coulomb caught the limp body between them, lowered him to the platform. The eerie gale ceased as quickly as it had begun.

All told, it had been less than three minutes since Tempest stepped up before the crowd.

Mentaxa, looking woozy, leaned on De' Artveldt's proffered arm. "I put him to sleep. It was the quickest thing I could think of."

"You did good work, child," De' Artveldt said.

Mimic had security duty for the day; Coulomb heard his whisper on the private channel. "Mimic has ordered an ambulance. It will arrive at the landing pad in moments."

Bolt, meanwhile, stepped forward and raised her hands. "Hey, kids, *grip!* The danger's over. Settle down now."

Slowly, the panic subsided and the crowd settled. "I guess," Bolt went on, "some people just weren't meant to be PsiScouts." That got a laugh.

Legion's body blurred, split, and there were three. Two of them lifted the unconscious Tempest between them.

"Do you need help?" Coulomb asked, feeling awkward.

"No thanks," the two Legions answered in unison. "You stay for the rest of the show. We'll get him to the mediplex."

Legion's two dopplegangers entered Headquarters, the doors snapping solidly shut behind them. Overhead, Coulomb saw an ambulance, red lights flashing as it settled to touch Liberty's upreaching hand.

Colossus was back to normal size, and Bolt had the audience calmed down. "I guess you can see that life as a PsiScout isn't all fun and games," she said. "An untrained psionic is dangerous to everyone, including themselves. That's one of the things we Scouts are out to do—to see that people like Tempest get the help they need to learn how to deal with their abilities."

"What's going to happen to him?" a voice called out.

"Legion is taking him to the mediplex. Depending on what the doctors say, we'll either enroll him as a Cadet, or we'll see that he gets whatever medpsych can help." She shook her head. "Enough of that now. Who's the next candidate?"

A plump girl clambered onstage. "That's a hard act to follow," she said, blushing.

"Please don't try to outdo him." Another laugh. "What's your name, and what do you do?"

The girl looked down. "I'm Tevichi Nowles. I haven't made up a PsiScouts name for myself. I didn't know we were supposed to."

Bolt grinned. "Tevichi is fine. What's your ability?"

"Uh...well, watch." Tevichi bowed her head, crossed her arms over her chest. For nearly a minute, nothing at all happened, and there were titters from the crowd.

Tevichi looked up, red as sunset. "I'm s-sorry. Sometimes it takes a little w-while."

Fade hissed at the audience. "Ain't easy doin' what she's doin'. Maybe ye'd like to be up here instead? Give girl a break." She faced Tevichi. "Ye just takes ye time, Tevi."

Again Tevichi bowed her head, and Coulomb heard her softly humming to herself. It was difficult, he knew, to produce psi abilities on demand. Take it easy, girl, he thought. Relax.

Abruptly, as if she were a volunteer in a magician's act, Tevichi Nowles rose into the air. A few centimeters at first, then a meter, two, three...until she was six meters above the crowd, floating as peacefully and effortlessly as a cloud. Grinning now, she spread her arms, pitched forward, and flew.

During the next ten minutes, the crowd and the PsiScouts alike gasped, giggled, and sighed as Tevichi swooped, now touching Liberty's crown, now skimming the waves, now buzzing the Scouts on their platform. Finally she came to a landing, settling softly as a fallen leaf to the platform before Bolt with her arms raised in a gesture of triumph.

"Excellent!" Bolt said. "So you're psychokinetic?"

"Only as far as flying goes."

"Your control is obvious. What about speed, altitude, and such?"

"Uh...I haven't exactly clocked myself, but I can outrace a car. I don't seem to have any altitude limits besides needing to breathe. And it gets pretty cold up there."

Mentaxa frowned, and Coulomb caught a spillage of her thoughts: *If she has that much trouble starting up, what's going to happen when we really need her?* He wasn't sure how tightly Mentaxa was directing her thought, or if Tevichi had picked up on it. Whatever the cause, the flier blushed again.

Bolt reached into a pocket and handed Tevichi a PsiScouts patch. "You gave a good demonstration, Tevichi. We're not going to make any decisions until we've seen all the candidates, but you should be proud of yourself." Dismissed, the other girl returned to the crowd.

"All right," Bolt said, "Who's next?"

❖

Six hours. It had taken that long to finish screening all the candidates and get rid of the audience—most of whom were in the mood to party. The sun was sinking when the Scouts finally assembled in the conference room.

Coulomb's head swam. He'd seen everything. Kids who flew, kids who glowed green, kids who created a deep-freeze with the wave of a hand. Girls who controlled animals and boys who breathed underwater. Kids who lifted ton-lots of scrap metal, kids who made trees dance, even one kid who could flatten himself into a two-dimensional shadow.

Whom to pick?

"I liked the flying girl." Legion punched at his terminal. "Tevichi."

Mentaxa snorted. "Useless." She punched up image after image, tiny simulacra of the day's candidates that followed one another across the table in front of her. "Useless, useless, useless. Unreliable, unpracticed, untalented."

"It's not their fault," Colossus said, "that their talents don't work as consistently as ours."

Bolt held up a hand. "We're not saying it's anyone's *fault*. But I think everyone has to agree that these kids all need practice."

Fade shivered. "What if cold-girl's power had run amuck the same way Tempest's did? Absolute Zero. PsiScouts on ice."

Colossus leaned back in his chair with a frown. "What's the matter? Is the club getting too crowded?"

Fade met his eyes. "What that supposed to mean, Big Boy?"

"Well, just speaking as a recently-admitted outsider, it seems like it can be pretty hard to join the PsiScouts. Maybe *too* hard. And maybe that's deliberate."

Fade stuck out her tongue. "Can't be too hard if we took *ye.*"

"Yeah, well, maybe you'd—"

"Enough!" Bolt's eyes flashed. "Do your bickering on your own time. Act like PsiScouts for now."

Mimic cleared his throat. "Mimic thinks that we can conduct discussions calmly and rationally. He wants to hear from Legion how candidate Tempest is doing."

Legion shrugged. "He's still unconscious. One of my duplicates is standing by at the mediplex until he's awake. The doctors don't know what to make of him." The boy frowned. "There aren't that many specialists in the medical conditions associated with psi. Maybe we should talk to De' Artveldt about trying to attract some."

Bolt nodded. "That's an excellent idea. Would you take care of that? Colossus, can I ask you to help Legion?"

Colossus shifted uncomfortably in his chair. "I guess so. All right."

"Good. Now what are we going to do about the candidates?"

Coulomb looked from face to face. "We're all pretty tired after today. I know I'm not feeling my best. Is there any reason we can't sleep on it and come back to the question when we're fresh?" When tempers fade, he thought to himself.

Colossus sighed. "No, hold on. I think we can settle it now. It wouldn't be fair to keep the candidates waiting." He took a breath, looking sheepish. "Y'all are right, none of those kids is really ready. They could hurt someone—or themselves. I guess I was out of line." Turning to Fade, he offered his hand. "I apologize."

For a moment Fade looked as if she would refuse his apology, and Coulomb wondered what they would do if she did. Then, she flashed a grin and took Colossus's hand. "Ye're okay, Big Boy," she said. "Just don' want any of those teeners hurt, is all."

"Mimic suggests that we establish this group as the first cadre of Cadets. They need practice and training in using their psi talents." He lowered his eyes. "He also suggests that Colossus would be best to co-ordinate the Cadets."

Colossus looked alarmed. "Hey, I'm still new at this. Why not Fade or Legion?"

"We *all* be new, Big Boy. An' I got hands full enough with gangers. Can't take on new charges."

Legion shook his head. "I can help you out, Gery, but with the Irregulars and this new medical thing, even six of me isn't enough to handle the Cadets, too."

Coulomb leaned forward. "If you'll be in charge, Colossus, I'll be glad to help you out."

Colossus's face held simultaneous expressions of dread and resignation. "All right. But let me warn you, I expect all of you to take a turn with these kids. I might even decide on some sort of buddy system...and I don't want to hear complaints if I do."

"Fair enough," Bolt answered. "I'm sure you'll want to set up some training space; most of this building is free. And you'll need a budget: talk to De' Artveldt about that. I'm sure she'll give you whatever you need."

"Isn't she afraid that we'll bankrupt her?"

"She says she has so much money that even we couldn't spend it all."

"Fun to try, though," Mentaxa said.

"Gery, one more thing," Bolt continued. "All of us here need to keep working on our Talents. We're none of us as strong or reliable as we could be. In addition to working with the Cadets, I'd appreciate it if you'd set up some kind of training schedule for the rest of us." She looked around the table. "And I'd appreciate it if we could all keep to that schedule."

Fade stuck her tongue out, then turned translucent as Bolt balled up a piece of paper and threw it at her. It hit the back of Fade's chair and dropped to the floor.

Bolt shook her head in mock sorrow. "I guess we're done for now. Unless anyone has any other business?" She waited, but no one spoke up. "Okay. I'll call De' Jenthen and get her to call a press conference to announce our decision, and—"

A loud wail interrupted her: the priority signal of an incoming call from Earth Police Chief Ormandeau's office. Bolt looked toward Mimic, who caught her eye on him and shrugged. "What?"

"You're on security duty, lumphead," Colossus said. "Answer it."

"Oh. Mimic forgot." He punched his communit; the alarm went silent and an image of Chief Ormandeau's unlovely face formed above the conference table. "PsiScouts," Mimic uselessly supplied.

"I didn't think I'd be calling on you kids this soon," Ormandeau growled. "We have a situation that needs your... unique talents."

Bolt leaned forward. "What's down?"

"You're all familiar with the Institute for Temporal Studies?"

Coulomb had never heard of the place, but his suit's computer fed him information quickly, words and numbers racing across the bottom of his visual field.

"Princeton," Fade said. "Eggheads think they can time travel. Tight security." Her tone suggested firsthand experience with the place, and not for the first time Coulomb wondered what Fade had been doing before she joined the Scouts.

"Exactly. We've just had a distress call from the Institute. It seems that they have intruders and they've asked for our help in dealing with them. They specified that the intruders exhibit paranormal abilities." Ormandeau shrugged. "You're the closest thing we have to a paranormal response squad...so you're it."

"Right," Bolt answered. "We'll pick up additional information *en route*."

"How are you getting there?"

Bolt blushed. "Oh. Er...Chief, I don't suppose you could send a car for us?"

"*All* of you?"

She looked around the table, the came to a decision. "Yes. We don't know what kind of Talents we might need."

Chief Ormandeau shook his head. "Now I've heard everything. All right, a car will be there in minutes. See that you're ready."

❖

The police driver introduced himself as Officer Ched A'run. He was a redhead, only a few years older than most of the Scouts, and he seemed to know all about them. There was barely room for all seven teeners plus Officer A'run; Bolt and Coulomb crowded together in the front seat while the other four sat in back. After they'd cleared New York and been underway for a few minutes, Mimic said, "Mimic cannot take any more of this togetherness," and transformed into a small mouse. Perched on Colossus's shoulder, he endured the rest of the trip in silence.

Bolt tried to contact the Temporal Institute, but was answered only by an uninspiring autosec which refused to connect her with a real person. "You'd think they could at least talk to us," Bolt fumed.

"Maybe they're too busy," Legion muttered.

"I'd rather not think about *that*," Colossus said.

"At least we have the layout of the place." By querying Princeton City's architectural database, Coulomb had managed to find the Institute's blueprints; he keyed for the display to appear on everyone's goggles and on the car's windshield. The complex was composed of many disconnected buildings, scattered across hectares of land and surrounded by a high fence.

"They sure don't want company," Legion observed.

"Which makes it all the more ominous that an intruder got in," said Mentaxa.

Bolt glanced at the dashboard readout. "We're supposed to go to something called the Chronotachyonics Lab," she said, stumbling over the unfamiliar term. "Ten creds to whoever finds it first."

"Building Twelve," Fade answered at once.

"Building Twelve it is, then." The car banked, and Coulomb saw the spires of Princeton below. The Temporal Institute was a few kilometers west of the town. "Legion, split in two before we go in. One of you, stay in the car and keep an ear on the commlink. The other, go with Colossus around to this back entrance." A blinking arrow on the map showed the doorway she meant. "I'll take Mentaxa and Coulomb in the front entrance. Fade, you follow us, invisible. Mimic, stay in your current form and ride in Colossus's pocket." She took a breath. "That gives us three aces in the hole in case we need them."

"Four," Officer A'run said, grinning. "I'll be in the car. If you need me, give a yell on the police freq." He patted the stunner holstered at his hip. "I'm a pretty good shot."

"Thanks," Bolt said. "We'll let you know."

"We're going in. Hold on."

Before the car even touched the ground, Coulomb sprang out. Bolt and Mentaxa joined him, while the others headed in the opposite direction. Although he couldn't see her, Coulomb knew that Fade was right behind him.

"All right," Bolt whispered, "Stay gripped and look professional." She led the way to the front door, which snapped open without even scanning them.

A two-and-a-half meter tall praying mantis, dressed in a white laboratory coat, met them with open arms.

"Greet-tinks." The creature's mandibles cut its words in two. "I am Sssirt-kat Sep-tim-musss, Chief Research-er. Wel-come to the Temporal Inssst-titute."

"Thank you. I'm Bolt, this is Coulomb and Mentaxa."

"Of the PsssiSsscoutsss. Yesss, I know. I asssked for you esssp-pecially. We have a bit of a prob-lem. Pleassse come thisss way."

Sssirt-kat Sep-tim-musss led the way to a large room filled with massive equipment that, to Coulomb, looked more impressive than the engines of the *Terran Queen*. Half a dozen robots, at least, seemed completely occupied in the task of maintaining the equipment. At the far end of the room was an oval opening about twice the height of a man; beyond it was an empty stage, and beyond *that* was a formless grey void that seemed to stretch away infinitely.

"Thisss isss our pri-mary lab. Here isss my asssisssst-ant, Ramu Fornix."

A young boy sat at a control panel facing the stage. He was dressed in a white lab coat, and where his skin showed it was pale green. Coulomb looked closer, and saw a fine tracery of silver lines on the boy's hands and arms. When Ramu Fornix turned to look at him, Coulomb saw that his face, too, had the same color and the same lines. His hair was short and dark, his eyes dark green and penetrating.

"An honor to make your acquaintance," he said with a nod. Coulomb noticed that conduits from the control panel were plugged into data sockets set in Fornix's wrists.

"You're an Aarnalian, aren't you?" Mentaxa asked.

"Yes," the boy answered, matter-of-factly.

"Aar-- which?" Coulomb echoed.

"I come from the planet Aarnal," answered Ramu Fornix. His voice, while not the toneless quality of a computer, was calm and quiet. "We are a civilization of sapient machines— living computers. I was grown in humanoid form to facilitate my interface with the Human peoples of the Galaxy."

"How old are you?"

"I emerged from the gestation chamber fifteen point three one standard years ago. I left Aarnal eight months ago, and have been attached to the Temporal Institute since." He blinked in a curiously machinelike way. "I am networked to the large databanks on Aarnal. There, I have access to one thousand six hundred fifty-three years of the recorded knowledge and experience of my race." A shrug. "I am sorry, but your question admits to no one simple answer."

"Could we swap life stories later?" Bolt shot Coulomb a hard look—entirely unjustified, he thought, since he'd only asked a couple of questions. It was the silver-green boy who had done all the talking.

Bolt turned back to Sssirt-kat Sep-tim-muss, squaring her shoulders in an attempt to look all-business. "You had an intruder?"

"We *have* an intruder," Ramu Fornix corrected.

"Ssshow themmm."

"Observe." Ramu Fornix nodded toward the stage, at the same time moving his hands over the controls before him.

For a moment it seemed as if iridescent colors swirled in the grey void, on the limit of sight. Then, as if an unseen curtain had parted, a man was standing there. He was hairless but not particularly old; his skin had an ochre tinge that was not entirely disagreeable. He wore tan robes and was barefoot. A heavy pendant, a green stone in an ornate gold setting, hung from a heavy golden chain against his chest.

The strangest thing about the man was that he stood frozen in a completely improbable pose, one foot stretched out behind him and one hand raised, his sleeve caught in mid-flutter and his mouth half-open. Coulomb assumed that he was seeing a still-frame holographic image.

"Asss you sssseee, we have isssolated the intruder in a ssstasssisss bubble. He isss arresssted in time, completely outsssside the normal sssequensssse of duration."

"You mean that *isn't* a hologram?" Bolt asked.

"Hardly," Ramu Fornix said. "Inside the stasis bubble, time does not pass relative to *our* time."

"When we detected the intruder, Ramu wasss able to power up the machinery and...catch him in the act. It wasss then that we sssummoned your assssissstanssse."

"What was he doing?"

"Why, I assssume that he wasss trying to sssteal our time machine."

Bolt rolled her eyes.

"Breaking and entering," Mentaxa said. "Trespassing. There's enough to take him in, anyway."

Ramu Fornix looked at her as one looks at a particularly clumsy and not-too-bright puppy. "You might," he said, "add conspiracy to commit murder, reckless endangerment of other sapients, and attempted genocide. He also copied all our files and schematics, which are classified by order of the Myriad Worlds."

Bolt didn't blink, but only asked Sssirt-kat Sep-tim-muss, "Will you confirm these charges?"

"Yesss."

"All right, then. We're going to take him in. Can we move him while he's in your stasis bubble?"

"Regrettably, no. It will be necessssary for usss to releassse him."

Bolt nodded. "I'll give the word. Mentaxa, be ready to subdue him if you need to. Cou, cuff him—but stay out of my line of fire."

Coulomb stepped forward, retrieving a pair of Earth Police standard-issue handcuffs from a pocket. They were strips of semi-rigid permaplast, each three centimeters wide and about ten long. When activated, they locked together over a prisoner's wrists and could not be released without a special tool at the precinct headquarters.

He stepped cautiously onto the stage, and felt a line of resistance like an invisible wall separating him from the suspect. After checking to see that he was not between Bolt and the man, he announced, "I'm ready."

"Mentaxa?"

"Ready."

"On three, then. One...two...THREE!"

Ramu Fornix threw a switch. As if a holo projector had been re-started, the man onstage jerked into motion. He looked from face to face, then slowly put his hands up. "I surrender," he said.

Coulomb moved forward cautiously, cuffs ready. The man met his eyes. "I'll cooperate. I don't think we really need those, do you?"

Coulomb looked toward Bolt. She frowned, then shook her head. "I guess it isn't necessary. As long as you'll come with us quietly, De'...?"

"I am Arras Pou-Dinh," the man supplied. "A humble disciple of the Morlex Disciplines." His voice was soft, soothing, grandfatherly. "I'm genuinely sorry to be the cause of such trouble."

"That's all right," Coulomb said, extending a hand to help De' Pou-Dinh off the stage.

"It is *not* all right," Mentaxa said. "He's hyp—"

Arras Pou-Dinh met Mentaxa's eyes and she froze. "My dear," he said, "you can't be upsetting the others. Why don't you sit down and relax while the rest of us settle this thing between us?"

Nodding her agreement, Mentaxa slumped into the empty seat next to Ramu Fornix. Yawning, she lowered her head and closed her eyes.

Resting a hand on Coulomb's shoulder, the old man gestured for him to leave the stage, and followed a step behind. Coulomb did as he was directed, and stopped next to Bolt. The cuffs dangled, forgotten, in his right hand. Bolt, too, seemed uncertain about what to do next; her hands were poised as if ready to throw electric bolts across the room, but she didn't move.

Pou-Dinh faced apparently-empty air and said softly, "You don't have to pretend not to be there, you know. Why don't you join the rest of us?" Amazingly, Fade shimmered into view, only half a meter from where Coulomb stood. Slack-jawed, she said, "Sorry."

"No offense taken." Pou-Dinh moved behind Ramu Fornix and looked over the boy's shoulder at the controls. "Now, let's see what settings will prove profitable."

Fornix glared, but seemed frozen in place. "You are a psionic hypnotist."

"How very astute. Yes, that *is* my native Talent. But years in the Morlex School taught me many other mental disciplines. And with the Star of Vidar," he touched the emerald pendant at his chest, "to augment my powers, controlling this small crowd is a simple matter indeed."

"You cannot hypnotize the massed overmind of Aarnal," Ramu Fornix said.

Pou-Dinh shook his head. "Oh, I'm sure. I *can*, however, hypnotize this shell of flesh and silicon which sits before me —at least for long enough to accomplish my aims." He glanced at Sssirt-kat Sep-tim-muss. "Doctor, tell me about the temporal Outriggers you've launched."

"We have disss-patched five tem-poral Outriggersss into the timessstream. We have maintained con-tact with three of them. Exact fixesss are available for all three."

"And where are they?"

"Outrigger Beta wasss sssent to the explossion of Thera in 1500 B.C; we believe it is encased in hardened lava at the bottom of the Mediter-ranean Sssea. Outrigger Gamma wasss sssent to the Tungusss-ka Event in 1908 and ssseemsss to have lodged in a Sssiberean hill. Our readingsss are mossst sssporadic. Outrigger Epsssilon wasss disss-patched to the Ketrus hypernova in the distant future."

"You do not leave an old man much choice. What is your margin of error with the Tunguska Outrigger?"

"Sssix hoursss, plusss or minusss."

Pou-Dinh tapped Ramu Fornix on the shoulder. "Open a temportal to six hours before the Tunguska blast. As soon as I am through, you will close the portal and randomize the settings."

His hands shaking as if palsied, the boy changed settings on the panel before him. On the stage, the infinitely-deep grey oval seemed to pulse, and then all at once it looked into the shadows of a forest.

"Thank you," Arras Pou-Dinh said, mounting the stage. "So sorry to be a bother." With that, he stepped through the portal and into the woods. An instant later, the portal collapsed with a thunderclap and the endless, featureless grey was back.

"Damn," said Ramu Fornix.

Coulomb shook his head, feeling as if he'd just awakened from a long sleep. Bolt, standing next to him, shivered. "What the *hell* just happened?"

"I fear that the sssit-uation isss not good. Not good at all."

Fade looked around, dazed. "What go down here?"

Bolt straightened her back. "Everybody grip for just a second. Cou, you all right?"

"I think so."

"Fade?"

"Confused."

"Mentaxa?"

Mentaxa, slumped in her seat, gave no answer. Her eyes were open but her jaw as limp and she seemed to be completely unaware of her surroundings. She looked even more pale than usual.

Bolt and Coulomb knelt next to her; Bolt took her hand. "Mentaxa? Iris, do you hear me?"

Gael? Mentaxa's telepathic voice seemed to come from kilometers away. *Royd?*

Right here. With her free hand, Bolt gripped Coulomb's shoulder so tightly that his suit stiffened protectively. *Come back to us.*

Hold on. Keep talking.

Damn it, Iris, we need you right here right now! Get back here and get your skinny butt up off that chair so you can help me deal with this crisis!

Coulomb was dimly aware that Fade, Ramu Fornix, and Sssirt-kat Sep-tim-muss had gathered around them, that Fade was talking into her commlink, summoning the others. *Mentaxa, we need you,* he thought, with as much clarity as he could muster.

Abruptly, Mentaxa convulsed, coughing. Then, gasping deeply, she said, "I'm okay. I'm all right."

Really?

Really. I wasn't ready for him, that's all. I guess I still have a little bit to learn about being a telepath.

Bolt squeezed her hand, then stood. "She'll be all right. Let's give her some room."

By this time, the other Scouts were storming through the door, accompanied by Legion's second self and Officer A'run. Colossus, in the lead, stopped and surveyed their faces. "What happened?"

"That's what we all want to know." Bolt turned to Sssirt-kat Sep-tim-muss. "Doctor, can you explain this so that we can all understand?"

The insectoid scientist bobbed its head. "Thisss isss a calamity. That creature jussst transss-ported himsssself into the remote passst. Into the year 1908, to be precissse."

"So what calamity?" asked Fade. "Bad guy in the past. Out of our hair."

"No, no, no, you do not under-ssstand. If Arrasss Pou-Dinh were to change hisss-tory, the con-sssequencccesss would be disssasssstrousss. Sssupossse he inter-ferred with early ssspacccce travel, or prevent-ed the formation of the Myrad Worldsss?" The scientist's antennae twitched violently. "The harm isss incalc-ulable."

"Not quite incalculable." The green boy, Ramu Fornix, was staring straight ahead as if looking beyond the lab.

"According to the calculations of Aarnal, if Arras Pou-Dinh pursues the optimum strategy, he has an eighty-seven point three six percent chance to succeed in establishing interstellar warp travel on Earth prior to the close of the Twentieth Century, and well before Earth society has matured sufficiently. A warlike Earth culture will expand through the Galaxy and there will be centuries of conflict. With time-travel at his disposal, Arras Pou-Dinh will return to a bloodstained present in which the Myriad Worlds are ruled by a single tyrannical overlord. With the way prepared by folklore and superstition that he, himself, will have planted in the past, Arras Pou-Dinh will become that tyrant."

Bolt's mouth hung open; she closed it slowly, then shook her head. "Wait, now. Just wait a second. You mean he's going make changes...what? Five hundred years ago? And today's world will change, poof, just like that?"

"I asssure you, my friend, that isss exact-ly what will happen. Perhapsss not ssso quick-ly asss that."

"How soon?"

"There isss a vassst temporal inertia involved. Many threadsss of hissstory mussst re-weave themsssselvessss. For a time, there will be chaosss asss the framework of reality adjussstsss. Sssmall thingsss are changing even asss we ssspeak. We do not notissse, becaussse our memoriesss are alssso adjussssted." The scientist shrugged. "Hoursss, daysss. No longer than that. Perhapsss lessss."

Bolt took a breath. "How can we stop him?"

"There isss no way. Even if you returned to the passst, you would arrive too late to prevent change."

Colossus said through clenched teeth, "Send us back to the same time you sent him. We'll stop him." He pounded his fist into the opposite palm.

"That will not work. We cannot sssend you to the sssame temporal locussss."

"Why not?"

Ramu Fornix looked over his shoulder, his eyes now focused on the room. "We cannot just send you anywhere in history that you desire. We need a stable locus that we can get a fix on. The best locus is one of our temporal Outriggers—of which three are currently in operation."

"Like taking the subway?" Coulomb volunteered. "You can only get off where there's a station, not in the middle of the line."

Ramu Fornix considered for a moment, then nodded. "The analogy is useful. Yes, Mimic?"

"How did the Outriggers get there in the first place?"

"A concentrated release of great energy can also serve as a temporal locus. With scanners on this end, we can get a fix on volcanic eruptions, earthquakes, fusion blasts, other catastrophic events. That fix is usually stable enough for us to send a Outrigger."

Mentaxa nodded. "The eruption of Thera in 1500 B.C. The Tunguska comet impact in 1908. The Three-Minute War."

"Yes. Our Tunguska Outrigger arrived shortly before the impact—which it survived in a stasis bubble—and was giving sporadic signals for most of the Twentieth Century before it was destroyed by mining equipment. Arras Pou-Dinh caused himself to be temported to its earliest location, six hours before the blast." He glanced at the controls. "Now, I am not receiving signals from that Outrigger. I assume he adjusted its frequency so that we can no longer use it as a locus."

"So there are only two times we *can* go?"

"Right now, yes. The Iron-Age Mediterranean, or the Ketrus hypernova."

Sssirt-kat Sep-tim-muss spread its limbs. "And you sssee, neither of thossse isss any help in ap-prehending Arras Pou-Dinh. Disssassster, pure and sssimple."

"Ketrus," Bolt mused. "Suppose we could get the Ketrus Outrigger to Earth? Then you can use it to get a fix and send us there?"

"In theory, yesss. But—"

Bolt was grinning. "One object *did* warp from Ketrus to Earth just before that hypernova."

Mentaxa whistled, and Coulomb felt a chill.

It was the most famous journey in history—and the most tragic story in the Galaxy. A million years in the future, the last remnants of the Human race lived in half a dozen planetary systems scattered across a hundred parsecs. On the world Ketrus, opposing factions battled in a thousand-year war whose origins they'd forgotten.

A group of pacifist scientists gathered in the name of sanity to save what was left of their peoples and culture. As they worked, the war intensified—finally, one side launched the doomsday weapon, the Starcracker bomb that turned their sun into a hypernova. All life in an entire sector of the Galaxy was destroyed—including the final Humans.

Moments before the end, an experimental warp-drive ship left, carrying the accumulated records of a ten-thousand-year civilization, the recorded memories of the scientific team... and the most precious cargo of all, a bio-capsule bearing the last child of Humanity.

Warped a million years into the past, the ship reached twentieth century Earth, where it was was found by a young married couple who had just lost their first baby. The bio-capsule released its cargo—a boy with abilities beyond belief, his brain overlaid with the fused personalities of the greatest minds of the homeworld he had never known. When he was old enough, he took the Ketrussi name Ran-Arl: Star Child.

That infant, Ran-Arl, grew up to become Power Man, the very first of Earth's Champions...and the greatest, save one.

"Mimic thinks that Bolt has lost her mind."

Bolt ignored him. "All we've got to do is make sure that Outrigger gets aboard Ran-Arl's ship. We can do it—I *know* we can."

Legion's two selves chimed in, "Even if you *do* get there safely—"

"—Which we doubt—"

"—You'd never survive on Ketrus's surface—"

"—Because of the gravity—"

"—And the heat."

Bolt touched her suit. "That's exactly the sort of thing our suits are designed to protect us against."

Bolt was right; Coulomb's suit computer informed him that Ketrus's three gees and ambient temperature near boiling water would be no trouble for the suit's defenses.

Ramu Fornix gave a blank stare. "Aarnal says that what you propose is within the limits of possibility, if only barely." He blinked. "Further, if we are to take action, we must do so quickly. Aarnal is not sure how much longer we will retain time-travel capability at all."

Bolt stepped onto the stage. "It's settled. We have to try. Who's with me?"

Coulomb stepped forward. "For a chance to see Ketrus, and maybe twentieth century Earth? I'm in."

Mentaxa shrugged. "I have a score to settle. And a telepath will be helpful."

Fade tossed her head. "You three crazy. Come on, Legion —time to write procedures for dealing with dead Scouts."

"M-Mimic thinks that his abilities would probably be useful on this mission. H-He is wwilling to go along."

He's scared to death, Mentaxa signaled.

Bolt shook her head. "Everybody can't go. If the Doctor is right, things are going to start coming apart here at home. We need someone to stay and try to hold it together." She surveyed the others. "Me, Mentaxa, and Coulomb. The rest of you, do your best." She mounted the stage. "Ramu, we're wasting time. What do we need to know about this machine?"

Ramu Fornix detached himself from the control panel and stood. "Time travel is not like riding a jetboard. There is not enough time to teach you everything you must know." A gentle sigh. "I shall accompany you to operate the controls and keep you out of trouble."

Bolt grinned. "Fine. Fade, you're in charge until we get back."

"*If,*" was Fade's only answer.

Ramu Fornix hopped onto the stage, followed by Mentaxa. Coulomb stumbled after them. Was this a stupid thing to do? What if they never got back? What if they failed, and had to return to a universe ruled by Arras Pou-Dinh, a universe in which there was very likely *no* PsiScouts at all?

What if they never *tried*?

Stupid or not, this was all they could do.

Ramu Fornix held up a small sphere about the size of a soccer ball, but studded with blinking displays, keys, and switches. He released it, and it hovered before him at chest-height. "Most of the temporal displacement equipment is located in hyperspace; this is the master unit's extension into normal space. It will follow us where and when we travel." He made a face. "Doctor Sssirt-kat, who fancies that it resembles a piece of ornamental jewelry, calls it the Time Bauble." He pulled a cable from the sphere and plugged the cable into his wrist. "I will now establish a stasis bubble, removing us from the normal flow of time."

Room, stage, and all vanished, replaced by an in-curving mirrored surface, a spherical wall about four meters across. Coulomb stared at his own distorted reflection, smeared out across a quarter of the sphere.

Mentaxa shivered. "I can't sense any thought patterns besides us four. It's as if we're all alone in the universe."

"We are," Ramu Fornix agreed. "We are in our own hyperspatial domain. I am no longer in contact with the overmind of Aarnal, just as you are no longer in contact with the massed minds of Earth."

"What's it like outside?" Bolt reached toward the mirrored wall; it was just beyond her reach.

"There *is* no outside," Ramu Fornix said.

Coulomb felt a great silence, an emptiness, nothingness like the endless expanse of dreamless sleep. He strained his ears, and all he could hear was the gentle sound of breathing, and the rush of his own blood soft as incoming surf.

"Enough," Ramu Fornix said, breaking the spell. "If I am damaged, you will need to know this." He pointed to the Bauble. "Press this key, wait two seconds, then press these three all at once. You will need to use two hands, or the thumb, middle finger, and least finger of one hand." As he demonstrated, Coulomb noticed that Ramu Fornix had six fingers on each hand; the sixth was a second opposable thumb. That, he thought, would be a handy thing to have. "When you do this, the device will reset all its parameters to their programmed relative zero values. At that point, you and anything else within a two-meter radius will be translated back to the Temporal Institute at the moment of our departure." He blinked. "Obviously, this procedure is a last-resort operation."

"What if we're separated?"

"Here." He removed three little nubs, each about the size of a raisin, from the Bauble and handed one to each of the PsiScouts. "Keep this on your person. It is a micro-tracker that will allow the system to locate you in time and space."

Coulomb tucked the nub into a pocket inside the lapel of his suit, and sealed the pocket securely.

"I will now shift the co-ordinates to the earliest fix we have on Outrigger Epsilon. That should be roughly five years before the hypernova that destroyed Ketrus." Ramu Fornix closed his eyes, and his brow wrinkled. "Yes. I have the fix. Executing."

A coruscating rainbow raced across the mirrored surface, at once painfully dazzling and achingly beautiful. The intense colors made Coulomb's eyes water, and his suit quickly established a polarizing field across his line of sight.

As quickly as it had come, the rainbow was gone, replaced by the deep star-strewn black of space. Coulomb heard a gasp, turned, and beheld a giant planet that filled half the sky. The blues, greens, and whites of Taarla or Earth were replaced here by a more somber palette of purples, violets, and reds. Two tiny moons shone over broad carmine oceans, and an enormous crimson sun burned like an ember in the dark.

"Ketrus," Ramu Fornix said. "The date, according to the Earth calendar, is May 9, 1,629,453. We are more than a million years in our own future."

"You sound oddly relieved," Mentaxa said.

"Time travel has yet to be tested on sapient subjects. All our results indicated that it would work, but still one has... uncertainties."

"All right," Bolt said, "We're...what? About five years before the supernova? Where is the Outrigger?"

"I have an accurate fix on the temporal Outrigger. It is on the surface of Ketrus's larger moon, ten thousand six hundred fifteen kilometers from us at the moment."

"And we can move to any point in the Outrigger's future?"

Ramu Fornix frowned. "The Outrigger's telemetry indicates that I must make some minor adjustments before we can do so. Perhaps it was damaged slightly in landing."

"So why are we still up here?"

"An excellent question. Prepare for phase-transition."

Before Coulomb could ask *how* he was supposed to prepare, his stomach lurched and the view shifted. They were above the moon, falling and spinning at the same time, the landscape wildly out of control. Coulomb felt his legs go out from under him, and fell heavily against the invisible, unyielding floor.

Through clenched teeth, Ramu Fornix grunted, "There... seems to be...something...wrong."

"I'll say!" Coulomb heard Mentaxa agree. Then Bolt fell on top of him, and the world went black.

❖

In the last two year, Ut Napis had been just about everywhere worth visiting.

It wasn't unusual for a teenager from Ixtal to warpfit an old jalopy and go cruising the stars in search of adventure. Everybody did it, usually right after finishing their formal schooling. It was tradition.

What *was* unusual was that Ut Napis kept at it long after other kids gave up and returned home. He knew he was unusual, because his mother didn't hesitate to tell him so, at great length, in every commo he got from her. The Kcheled boy, a year younger than Ut, had settled down into a highly lucrative career with one of the great biobusinesses. Cin Soreth, the proverbial girl next door, returned from her *wanderjahr* months ago, and was making plans for her wedding. Even Cousin Zorel (he *hated* Cousin Zorel!) was back at home, looking for a job.

Ut took a reading from the navicomp and smiled. Let them all go crawling back to Ixtal, to settle in like sessile *blad*-fish, building the careers and homes and families that would keep them anchored to homesoil until they died and were covered with it at last! Ut didn't care. He liked traveling, liked adventuring, and no one was going to make him give it up before he was good and ready.

After all, he thought, he'd seen things that no one on Ixtal had ever seen. As his journeys took him further and further into the galaxy, well beyond the bounds of the familiar Five Worlds, he'd visited planets ever-more-alien and cultures ever-less-familiar. He'd seen sights that bordered on incredible, had met and talked to creatures he never knew existed. And he'd learned far more than he ever did in school.

Ixtal was an ancient world, with an ancient culture and a long history of somnolent peace stretching back to long-lost Earth. There were no surprises, no danger, no thrills. No uncertainties. Nothing, in fact, that Ut enjoyed.

Take this latest trip, for example. No one on Ixtal ever wondered about the legendary lost colony. To them, Ketrus wasn't even a dream or a fable—it was irrelevant data, primitive superstition, a children's bedtime story. They would never think the actually go *looking* for Ketrus, just to see if it was there, just to see if it could be done.

But Ut was close, so close. He'd followed the millennia-old trail across kiloparsecs, scoured the folklore and astronomical records of a dozen alien civilizations, until now he was sure he'd found the right star system. That red giant ahead, a hundred million kilometers across and barely visible from more than five parsecs—so very much like the sun of home. He could see those long-ago colonists, lost in space and despairing, rejoice as they passed the shrouding dust clouds and saw this crimson oasis looming ahead. And then to find out that it had a nice, large planet already teeming with life! Of *course* they would have chosen to settle there.

Grinning, Ut Napis set his warpdrive controls, and punched the button.

❧

The ship slewed violently, instruments going wild, and Ut knew he was in trouble.

Outside the viewports he saw, not the usual soothing blankness of warpspace, but instead a dizzying riot of color and motion. He punched abort codes, but the ship didn't respond—some external force was in control of his warpfield, and it was throwing his ship about like a leaf in a storm. In all his travels, Ut had never encountered anything remotely like this.

There came a brutal lurch, which nearly threw him from his seat despite his anticrash belts. When he came to his senses, he realized that he was no longer in space.

His ship rested at a thirty-degree angle on a bright, stark landscape of black and grey; overhead, the stars were washed out by reflected sunlight, leaving the sky inky black. The gravity was weak, less than a tenth that of home. An airless moon, then, or a minor planet adrift in space.

Ut's main display was filled with null symbols; he swatted it and the unit cleared. A second later, status figures painted themselves across the screen and he whistled. The warpdrive was busted but good; the computer couldn't even make a preliminary diagnosis, because it couldn't get the warpdrive unit to answer its signals. It postulated that the unit's circuits might have been fried, and suggested an EVA to take a look.

Ut turned his attention to the environmental readings. A small, airless moon all right—grav just three percent, ambient temperature near the boiling point of lead. And something else—his ship was losing air and life-support. The system was working on repairing itself, but the computer strongly suggested he go on tanked air. If he intended to go outside, it added, he should wear a thermsuit to shield him from the sun.

"Like I have any choice," he muttered, undogging his straps and pulling a folded thermsuit from a locker. "I'll tell you one thing," he said in the direction of the computer, "if that backup warpdrive isn't working, I am not going to be a happy pilot." Breathing mask in place, he stepped into the airlock and punched the cycle button.

The inner door slammed, and Ut felt pressure drop around him. Vacuum didn't particularly bother him—Ixtallese skin was tough enough to make a pretty good space suit, at least for a few hours at a time. The sun was more of a worry: without the thermsuit, he would cook in his own juices long before the low pressure got to him.

The outer door swung open partway, then wedged against the ground. Ut shouldered past it, out onto the moon's surface.

He stopped dead in his tracks. A welcoming committee was waiting for him.

Four humanoids, three of them in matching pressure suits and the other one mostly-hidden behind a polarization field, stood before a towering machine that looked like a cross between a radiotelescope dish and a spinning wheel. The one in the polarization field was engrossed in examining the machine.

In Ut's ear, his commchip signaled that it was receiving a signal. All that emerged, though, was gibberish...albeit gibberish that seemed to bear a nodding resemblance to Galangua. It was coming from the tallest of the humanoids.

"Do you speak Galangua?" he asked. Most spacefarers— or, at least, their translation programs—could deal with the *lingua franca* of the galaxy. If that didn't work, he would try Ixtallese, although he doubted that these frail-looking creatures were the descendants of the Ketrus colony.

"Our translators can skriddy it well enough. Who are you?"

"Ut Napis of Ixtal. And you?"

The humanoids exchanged glances. "Bolt, Coulomb, and Mentaxa of Terra, and this is Ramu Fornix of Aarnal. Why did you bring us here?"

Ut sputtered. "Hey, *I* didn't bring *you* here. I was minding my own business when your crazy machine pulled me out of warp and dropped me here. I'm out one warpdrive, and if my spare isn't working then I'm going to hold all of you responsible."

"There's been a misunderstanding. We just arrived here. Apparently this machine pulled us out of...er...warp as well."

Ut put his hands on his hips. "So then who brought us here?"

From behind his ship came a cough, and another spacesuited humanoid emerged. This one was tall enough and bulky enough to be a Ketrussi, if indeed they were anywhere near Ketrus.

"I must apologize," the newcomer said. "I'm afraid that my experimental warp drive has caught all of you."

"And who are *you*?" Ut demanded.

The figure bowed. "Forgive me, I should have introduced myself right away. I am Do-Kar of Ketrus, scientist."

❖

Coulomb felt his throat go dry and his knees get weak. Do-Kar—the leader of the Ketrussi scientists, and the man who invented the warp drive! Talking about time travel was one thing, but it was something else entirely to be standing here, up to your ankles in powdery regolith, face-to-face with the tragic hero to beat all tragic heroes. Do-Kar saw the end of the world coming, begged for peace, and in return had been ignored and reviled. He labored to save that unwitting world, frustrated by fate at every turn, and died thinking himself a failure. Yet the tiny bit he *had* saved, Ran-Arl, had gone on to become a great and successful Champion and the key to the survival of the Ketrussi people.

Meekly, Coulomb and the other PsiScouts followed as Do-Kar took them down a sloping tunnel to his combination laboratory/home, carved into lunar bedrock about half a kilometer from the warp driver. Once inside, Ut Napis shed his thermal suit and breathing apparatus readily—but after one breath of the heavy, hot Ketrussi air, Coulomb and the others decided to retain their protective gear.

A tall, lovely Ketrussi woman introduced herself as Lur-Tela and sat them down in a spacious living room. "My husband and I," she said, "are not used to visitors." Particularly, her eyes seemed to say, alien ones. "We work alone here; the Military Council Technologic does not favor our experiments."

"You're trying to build a warpdrive," Ut Napis said.

"Yes," Do-Kar answered. "We have monitored hyperwave signals from spacefaring races, so we know such a drive is possible. As you can see, though," he spread his hands, "I have not yet mastered the technique."

"You're welcome to look over my drive," Ut Napis said. "I don't know how much you'll learn from it; I'm afraid the accident destroyed some circuits." He looked, pointedly and expectantly, toward Bolt.

She took a breath. "Our own warpdrive is also an experimental model. I'm sure Ramu will correct me if I'm wrong, but as I understand it, most of the actual equipment exists only in hyperspace. Our Outrigger, which provides a target for our drive, is lost. We have reason to believe it's on this moon."

Ramu Fornix nodded. "I believe I can locate the Outrigger. I am also fairly familiar with the theory of warpdrive engineering, and can assist you in repairing the damaged units."

"If you don't mind being our guests for a while," Do-Kar said, "this has been a long day for me. I'd just as soon put off work until tomorrow."

Everyone agreed. Do-Kar busied himself with preparing a meal, while Lur-Tela visited.

Lur-Tela, as it turned out, was an astronaut—one of the first in Ketrus's infant interplanetary program. She'd been the third person to walk on this very moon, and her marriage to popular scientist Do-Kar was cause for the whole planet to rejoice. Since then, the couple's stock with the public had fallen as Do-Kar tried to convince everyone that Ketrus's endless and ever-accelerating arms race had to end.

"They don't want to believe him," she said, "and so they don't allow themselves to listen. The fools don't know what danger they're in."

There was a painful silence and then Ran-Arl called, "Come to table, everyone."

Around the small table, the two adults and five teeners joined hands. "In the name of Krin who kindled the sun, and Ardene who lit the moons, we show our thanks. May we who sup here together be blessed with fortune and joy."

Ut Napis fell to the repast as if he hadn't eaten for weeks. Ramu Fornix passed a hand over each dish, then indicated three in particular. "These contain proteins that are poisonous to Humans. All the others, while nutritionally neutral, can safely be consumed. Pass food slowly through your suit's atmosphere field. You are well advised to take a few nutricapsules in addition to your meal."

The Ketrussi food was hot, and the tastes were unfamiliar. There was a green jelly that Coulomb could barely keep down, and something blue and breadlike that had all the flavor of sawdust. However, some of the greens were delicious, and there was a crunchy brown cracker that made him close his eyes and sigh in delight.

Ut Napis explained that he was from Ixtal, the homeworld from which the Ketrussi race had sprung a hundred centuries ago. A million years ago in the twenty-sixth century, Coulomb knew, Ixtal was an experimental Earth colony. Its inhabitants were a new breed of Humans, genetically engineered to thrive in heavy gravity and bathed in the infrared of a bloated red star. He wondered if Ut Napis was descended from one of those pioneers.

Probably, he decided.

"You say that your people have great fleets of starships?" Do-Kar said.

"There must be, I don't know, a million or more."

"I've been working on a warpdrive in order to build a fleet of evacuation ships, so that those of us who retain our senses can leave. Do...do you think your world could help us?"

Ut Napis met Do-Kar's eyes. "I don't want to make any promises. But if we repair my warpdrive, I'll return home and tell them about your wars. I can't see how the government could sit by and let a whole planet destroy itself."

"Then we must repair your warpdrive as soon as we can. We'll start tomorrow." He sighed. "My friends, I don't have much hope for our world. They don't want to hear. And if we

won't save ourselves, how can we expect others to do the job
for us?"

"Begging your pardon, sir," Bolt said, "but you're wrong.
You've got to keep on trying. It doesn't matter what the rest
of Ketrus believes or does—you know you're *right*. You know
you're doing the right thing. And you can't afford to wait
until the others choose to listen to you or believe in you—by
then it'll be too late."

"She's right, Kar," agreed Lur-Tela.

"I know," Do-Kar said. "It's just hard not to get
discouraged." He forced a smile. "Enough dreary talk. I want
to hear all about various adventures in space. This moon is as
far as any Ketrussi has ever traveled."

The evening passed quickly and happily as Ut Napis told
stories of his travels. Bolt and the other Scouts tried, as
gracefully as possible, to evade the questions of the others; in
general, she thought they succeeded fairly well. It helped that
they were very vague about the location of Terra and the rest
of the Myriad Worlds in relation to Ixtal and Ketrus.

Eventually, when everyone was yawning, Do-Kar showed
them to a an empty room off the main hall. "This is an
environmental control chamber; I'll set the air pressure and
temperature to levels that are more comfortable if you wish."

Bolt nodded. "That would be marvelous." Ramu reeled off
the settings that the humans preferred, then Do-Kar and Ut
Napis left, closing a heavy door behind them. The ventilation
system sighed, and Coulomb felt the air around him cool
deliciously. Soon, his suit softened around him and its
protective field dissolved.

"I still can't believe," Bolt said, "that we're actually here. I
mean *now*. It's like being in a holoshow."

"You needn't sound so delighted," Mentaxa said. "Don't
you have any compassion for these people? They have five
years of life…then it's all over. Can't we *do* something?"

Ramu shook his head. "Any changes that we introduce
into the timestream will alter our own world…possibly in

ways worse than the alterations that Arras Pou-Dinh has already introduced. History tells us that Ran-Arl, Power Man, was haunted all his life by the death of his people and his world. Their memories gave him a consciousness of loss and mortality which motivated him to heroism. Suppose we rescue Do-Kar and Lur-Tela from their fate—Ran-Arl will never exist, or will exist in a completely different form."

Coulomb sighed. "And without Power Man, Earth would be a cinder before the twenty-first century was over."

Mentaxa turned her face away. "All right, you've convinced me. We'll let them die."

"It's not just that," Bolt said. "We have to watch *everything* we say and do. Ramu, be careful how much warpdrive information you give Do-Kar. His drive was still in the experimental stage when Ketrus was destroyed."

"I will act with care. My historical database is unclear on the exact state of Ketrussi warp-physics at this time...I will know more when I have examined Do-Kar's machinery."

"What about Ut Napis?" Bolt frowned. "I don't remember him in the Power Man story."

"Sure you do," Coulomb prompted. "Only you know him as Do-San."

Bolt's eyes widened. "Power Maid's friend? The one who —oh!"

"Exactly. So you see, he isn't going to cause any trouble for us. I'm more concerned with finding the Outrigger, and how we're going to make sure it gets on Ran-Arl's ship."

"The Outrigger," Ramu said, "will be easy to locate using the time bauble. How we are to get it aboard a ship that is not yet even built is beyond me."

Bolt smiled. "Leave that to me...."

❖

Nicholas II, Tsar of All the Russias, felt secure and happy for the first time since he'd taken the crown. With Alexandra at his side and his son Alexei fully cured of his bleeding disease, he reigned over an empire prosperous and at peace from Kiev to Kamchatka. While the rest of Europe bloodied itself in a great war that started in the Balkans, Russia stayed wisely neutral and concentrated on putting her own house in order.

How much had changed in so little time. The Russian bear, somnolent and complacent for so many decades, was now awake and on the move. Affairs of state, once the exclusive province of the Tsar, were now shared more and more with the Duma and Nicholas' various ministers. As Nicholas loosened the reins, he saw his country becoming more of a constitutional monarchy like England. The people, peasants and aristocrats alike, were better fed and happier than they had ever been. Industry was on the march along the newly-completed Trans-Siberian Railroad, the arts flourished, and even the Marxists could find nothing to complain about since their leader, Vladimir Ilyich Ulyanov, had died in a French train wreck.

Nicholas and Russia owed all this great fortune to one man, a holy man who had emerged from Siberia when his country needed him the most: the monk Rasputin. Some called him a demon and whispered about the uncanny hypnotic power that lurked behind Rasputin's eyes; others called him a saint and praised God for his presence. Nicholas, who worked closely with Rasputin every day, knew that he was neither devil nor saint, but an ordinary man...the very embodiment of the common Russian peasant. Earthy, crafty, worldly-wise, uncomplicated—the man was worth any dozen other advisors. All Russia owed Rasputin a debt that she could never repay.

And now Rasputin was going away.

"I shall return, sire," the monk said. "Tell your son and his sons after him to look for me when their need is greatest."

"Then I'll never see you again?" Nicholas asked.

"No."

Nicholas knew that he should have felt sadness, but instead he experienced a kind of quiet joy. Wherever Rasputin was going, he was leaving Russia in good hands.

"I have said my farewells to the tsarina and tsarevich," Rasputin continued. "A parting gift for you, sire, and then I will take my leave." From his heavy cloak, Rasputin produced a gleaming, jewel-decked sphere such as the great Fabrege might have made. It was much larger than an egg, the size of a small melon, and intricate letters in some unfamiliar script covered every square inch that was not studded with gems. "See that you care for this well, Nicholas Alexandrovich. Place it in the deepest vaults, hide it from prying eyes, do not tell anyone where or what is it."

"What *is* it?"

"The future. Russia's future. This Outrigger is the key to the prosperity of your nation and your dynasty. Guard it well."

"I will." Nicholas took the object, which seemed to weigh almost nothing.

"And one more thing. In the vault in which you store this object, there must be a heavy door, securely locked—and you must leave a key to that door in the room with the Outrigger."

"Leave a key with the Outrigger." Rasputin's eyes bore deeply into Nicholas' very brain, and he felt that the monk was judging his inner soul. Satisfied, Rasputin nodded, looked away, and bowed. "Farewell, Nicholas." With that, he was gone.

❖

Ramu Fornix located Outrigger Epsilon in less than five minutes, using the time bauble and reading the settings directly into his bioelectronic brain. He asked Do-Kar for a map of the moon, and indicated the location of the Outrigger. "Handle it gently until I have a chance to inspect it and do whatever repairs are necessary," he told the others, then disappeared into Ut Napis' ship with Ut Napis and Do-Kar.

Bolt appealed to Lur-Tela for help.

The astronaut examined the map. "That's only about three hundred kilometers from here. An hour out and an hour back by skimmer."

"We don't know how to handle a skimmer," Bolt protested.

Lur-Tela smiled. "Not to worry. I'll take you. I haven't had a chance to go out on the surface for weeks. I need to see something besides these same walls and the telescreen."

Of course the trip lasted longer than two hours. There were many sights to see, and when they finally arrived at the site, the Outrigger was nowhere to be seen. They searched for the better part of an hour in the unrelieved sun, then gathered in the skimmer's shadow to plan their next move. Lur-Tela kicked at the thick layer of surface dust. "Perhaps your Outrigger is buried in the dust."

Bolt nodded. "I think you're right. I could wring Ramu's neck for sending us out here."

"Wouldn't do any good," Mentaxa said. "He probably doesn't need to breathe."

"I hate to go all the way back empty-handed," Bolt said.

"I can call Kar on the comm," Lur-Tela offered. "If he's not too engrossed in what he's doing, chances are even that he'll answer."

"I don't want to do that either." Bolt voiced her displeasure in a noise halfway between a hum and a growl. "He *knew* we wouldn't be able to find it. He just wants us to come back without it so he can sigh and act superior."

"Wait," said Coulomb. He stepped away from the skimmer, out into the sun, and raised his hands. Closing his eyes, he stretched out his magnetic senses, seeking within the powdered stone around him. There was the skimmer's engine, and its metallic hull. There were the suits of the others, their pressure fields like ice to the touch. There, like a far-off whisper, were the feeble traces of the moon's own rudimentary magnetic field.

Further.

A warp in the field, like a gentle hillock: some deep-buried iron, probably from a meteorite strike half a million years ago. A gradual swirl to the left, an arc of a thousand-kilometer curve: most likely a response to the changing density of the solar wind.

There!

A hard, hot knot in the moon's magnetic field, a small bit of substance that wove its own lines of flux like a cocoon around itself. He turned, opened his eyes, and pointed. "About three and a half kilometers that way. I'll know it when we get there."

They all set off in a loping run, and reached the Outrigger all together. It was the size of a small melon, studded with diodes and switches, three-quarters buried at the bottom of a five-meter depression in the dust. Bolt pulled it free and held it up triumphantly. "All right! Now we can go home."

On the ride back, Lur-Tela concentrated on flying the skimmer. When they arrived, the living quarters were empty; Do-Kar, Ut Napis, and Ramu Fornix were still busy with the partly-dismantled carcass of Ut Napis' warpdrive. It took firm persuasion to get the three to quit for the midday meal.

"I'm learning so much," Do-Kar said. "Just the chance to see a working warpdrive, based on an entirely different principle, is giving me ideas for my own design."

Lur-Tela smiled. "Then you'll be able to repair Ut's ship for him?"

Do-Kar's face fell. "Not quite yet."

"If ever," Ut Napis said. "The field coils are shot. I think we can work around that with stuff Do-Kar has here. And I can probably make do without most of the cybernetics, at least until I get to a planet that can replace my chips." He spread his hands. "But I don't know *what* I'm going to do for inertial compensators. Likewise the DEM circuits."

Ramu Fornix, examining the Outrigger, clicked his tongue a few times. "There is no help for it. You are going to have to go to Ketrus. From what Do-Kar says, there are a few manufacturers who produce adaptable equipment. You will have to look that equipment over in person and decide what best suits your purpose."

"My next scheduled trip to Ketrus is in a week," Do-Kar said. "I don't dare go sooner; the Military Council Technologic already suspects what I'm doing here. While I'm there, I'll talk to some of my equipment suppliers; you're welcome to come along and take a look at what we've got."

"Do you think it's safe?"

"Of course." Do-Kar nodded. "You look enough like a Ketrussi to pass. We'll tell people that you're a cousin. We'll call you...."

"Do-San," Lur-Tela volunteered.

"Yes. Do-San was the name of my older brother, Krin rest his soul. He died in a boating accident when we both were children. That's it, we shall introduce you as my cousin Do-San from Ranzz City."

Lur-Tela turned to Ramu Fornix. "What about *your* warpdrive?" She looked at the Scouts, and Coulomb was suddenly aware of his scrawny neck, his undermuscled torso and frail bones. Compared to the Ketrussi, any normal Human looked anorexic. "I'm afraid that none of you could pass for Ketrussi."

"No need," Ramu answered, holding up the Outrigger. "With a few hours in the workshop, I can adjust the Outrigger to function perfectly. I should be able to complete the work tonight, and then we can be on our way."

"We still need your help," Bolt said to Lur-Tela. "The Outrigger will stay behind to anchor our passage through hyperspace. Would you keep it safe for us?"

"Of course," Lur-Tela answered. "We'll be sorry to see you go. I know Kar will miss you."

"Our business is fairly urgent," Bolt said. "Maybe someday, if we can, we'll come back."

"Believe me," Mentaxa said drily, "you'll soon forget that we were even here."

"I doubt *that*," Do-Kar replied. "It isn't every day that we have alien visitors, you know."

Mentaxa gave no answer, merely exchanged a quick, knowing glance with Bolt. And Coulomb, watching the exchange, gave himself a mental boot to the head. So *that* was what they were planning! Of course!

Do-Kar finished his last bite and stood. "All right, let's get back to work on that drive. I think I have a way to safely reverse the polarity of the neutron flow."

❖

That night, the Scouts and Ramu Fornix were alone in their environment chamber while the rest of the household slept. Ramu produced the time bauble and touched it briefly to the Outrigger. "It's calibrated," he said. "I can transfer us to any time and place where this Outrigger exists."

"Earth?" Bolt asked.

Ramu frowned. "Uncertain. The timeline is stable up until the hypernova. Beyond that, there's a probability fog."

"Then we're not certain that the Outrigger will get aboard the survival ship."

"The probability wave will collapse to certainty once we take decisive action."

Mentaxa grunted. "You're putting the cart before the horse, and it's making my head hurt. Let's do it."

Coulomb glanced toward the door. "I hate to leave without saying goodbye."

Mentaxa pinned him with eyes that were deep pools of black. "When they wake up, they won't remember we were ever here. All they'll have is a compulsion to safeguard the Outrigger ."

Ramu nodded. "I do not see that this can damage the timestream."

"All right," Mentaxa said. "I'll do it." She closed her eyes and her face went slack. Long minutes went by, during which Coulomb tried not to stare at her but couldn't help himself. Finally, she shuddered and opened her eyes.

"There. I think it's done."

"Fine," said Bolt. "Now let's get out of here."

"Agreed." Ramu touched the time bauble. The air stilled, a hush fell, and a barely-visible curving transparency wrapped around them. "There. We are out of phase with the normal flow of time."

"Where do we go now? To Earth?"

Ramu shook his head. "The probability wave has not collapsed. It is still not established that the Outrigger reaches Earth." He took another reading. "I suggest that we move forward to the launch of the survival ship. Perhaps we can ensure that the Outrigger reaches its destination."

"There's something else I'd like to see first," Coulomb said softly.

"We aren't here to see the sights," Bolt said.

"I know. But I want to know what happens to Ut Napis."

Ramu frowned. "Yes, we can hover just out of phase and observe without being seen or affecting the timestream. An intermediate destination will give me a chance to test the system's responsiveness. Observe."

Ramu moved them upward, through layers of rock to the surface, then perched them next to Ut Napis' ship. Coulomb knew how Fade must feel.

Suddenly, all around them, time shifted into fast-forward. The sun, which had hardly moved at all during the two days of their visit, started creeping across the sky. Do-Kar, Lur-Tela, and Ut Napis appeared and withdrew, running madly, for periods of frantic work on the damaged engines. Then there came a time when Do-Kar and Ut Napis flew off in a skimmer, and only Lur-Tela was left.

"They're on Ketrus," Bolt said.

"I believe I could reconfigure the system to follow and observe them," Ramu offered.

"No. Let's just wait."

Soon, Do-Kar and Ut returned, laden with strange equipment. For three days they labored on Ut's engines, then vanished into the lab to emerge a good while later. All three entered the ship but only Do-Kar and Lur-Tela emerged. They retreated into the tunnel, then Ut's ship rose a few meters off the ground.

"They will attempt to use Do-Kar's warpdrive to launch Ut Napis toward civilization." Sure enough, Ut's ship hovered over the great antennae of Do-Kar's drive. "Unfortunately, Do-Kar's design is still defective. Observe...the drive opens a warpgate, and the ship proceeds into it." A ghostly hole in reality gaped before Ut's ship, which slid forward and was engulfed in unearthly colors. Instants later, the hole closed. "Fortunately, observations from this accident will enable Do-Kar to perfect his warpdrive design."

"What happened to Ut?"

"We know that there exists a natural equipotential line of warp flux between the present star systems of Ketrus and twentieth century Earth. Do-Kar's drive opened a warp gate along that line, and Ut Napis' ship has entered that gate. However, without means to open a corresponding gate on the Earth end, Ut Napis will remain in a warp potential field, a harmonic bouncing back and forth between Ketrus and Earth, past and future. He will not age nor perceive the passage of time."

"That's horrible. What can we do to get him out?"

"You are forgetting the Power Woman legend. Power Man's daughter, Zun-Kela, will be born in 1954. While examining the survival ship in 1969, Zun-Kela accidentally triggers the warpdrive and opens a warpgate. Ut Napis...or Do-San, as he will be called...materializes on Earth and is briefly befriended by Zun-Kela before he suffers his ultimate fate."

"And I guess we don't dare alter *that*, either?"

Ramu spread his hands. "The events are a matter of historical record."

Bolt glanced at the patch of sky where Ut's ship had vanished, then looked away. "We're not accomplishing anything here. Let's move on to right before the supernova, and do what we can to ensure that the Outrigger gets aboard that survival ship."

"As you wish." Ramu touched the time bauble, and the sky turned to brilliant rainbows.

❖

Do-Kar knew that it was the end.

A whole life spent studying, giving speeches, demanding, then pleading, then imploring. A life of plotting, maneuvering, hiding from the Military Council Technologic, struggling to make the fools see. A life, ultimately, of failure. And now, none of it mattered.

For Ketrus, it was too late. The Starkiller was triggered. The sun, for so many millennia a constant, unchanging circle of brilliant red, was shrinking in the sky, contracting and growing brighter, hotter, yellower. In another hour, two at most, the inward-falling shells of gas would hit a compression-wave and rebound, tearing the sun apart. If Ketrus wasn't baked to a cinder by then, the explosion would finish the job.

Lur-Tela squeezed his hand. "We've done what we could. More than anyone could have expected."

She was right. The gleaming survival ship, his last remaining prototype, was already loaded with two-thirds of its precious cargo. Its databanks carried all the knowledge and culture of the Ketrussi civilization. Eternal memory lattices—still being fed by sensors attached to Tela's and Kar's foreheads—held a gestalt of all the memories of every scientist in the compound. The ship would reach an inhabited planet, and preserve something of Ketrus.

Perhaps.

There would be other survivors. Convicted criminals and sociopaths, a score or more of them. They were now immaterial denizens of the Shadow Domain, an invisible, timeless extra-dimensional limbo that Do-Kar discovered as a byproduct of his early warpdrive design. There, inmates waited out their sentences in a gray nothingness, conscious but sensory-deprived. Now, they might linger forever, lost souls who were the last sons and daughters of dead Ketrus.

The Shadow Domain's usefulness to the Council—as a way to get rid of dissidents and troublemakers—allowed Do-Kar to continue his warpdrive experiments under the guise of improvements to the great machines that opened that realm. Do-Kar firmly believed that the only thing that kept him out of the Domain himself, was the fact that he alone knew the secret of its access.

"I should have started sending people into the Shadow Domain while it was still possible." Interference from the dying sun's raging atmosphere had made it impossible to open the gateway to the Domain. He had simply waited too long, and for that mistake he and all his friends would die.

Almost all.

He lifted the bio-capsule into the tiny ship's cargo space. The vessel was an ungainly contraption, little more than a packing crate festooned with antennae and welded to a fusion power supply unit...but it was a functioning starship. And with luck, it would carry Ketrus's last survivors to the safety of a far-He turned to Tela. "It's time to go, love."

Lur-Tela gripped his hand and shook her head. "No. I'm staying with you."

Their eyes met, and Do-Kar knew that her mind was made up, had been made up ever since the night they'd first discussed using the prototype as a lifeboat.

So be it.

"The bio-capsule will need more padding, then."

Tela clapped her hands, and a domestic robot rolled in laden with sheets, blankets, and pillows. "I already thought of that." Together, they piled the materials in the compartment, while Do-Kar's mind raced. The vessel's onboard computer was programmed to find a planet compatible with Ketrussi biochemistry. Since Ketrussi could live in anything from the dense oxy-ammonia mix of their own world to the stratospherically-thin oxy-nitrogen of other inhabited worlds and across a broad range of temperatures, the computer's parameters were wide indeed. Would it be enough? The bio-capsule's nano-technology was untried—would it preserve its precious cargo, Do-Kar and Lu-Tela's infant son? Could it transfer the collected memories of the scientists to the child? Do-Kar knew that there would be no sense of individuality, that all the memories were fused together into a single gestalt. Still, in one sense or another, somewhere in the cosmos, would they all live again?

"Anything else?" Do-Kar asked.

"Yes." Tela dashed across the room to a toolbox, rooted through, and triumphantly held up the Outrigger. The sensor-encrusted orb, a discarded piece of lab equipment, had been with them ever since the long-ago days on the moon. Lur-Tela considered it their good-luck charm.

She tucked the thing under a blanket, then turned away. Kar removed the sensor from her forehead. He gave one last prayer to Krinn, then detached his own sensor, and sealed the hatch before he could think better of it.

Taking Lur-Tela's hand, he closed a contact and backed away. Swiftly, silently, the ship rose through the open skylight and was lost in the ever-brightening sun.

❖

Coulomb wiped his eyes as the PsiScouts retreated into limbo, their view of Ketrus's last moments replaced by endless grey fog.

Ramu Fornix checked the time bauble and nodded. "I have a clear fix on the Outrigger," he announced. "As predicted, it reached Earth on March 25, 1927. I can take us to any time between then and November 1992." He glanced up. "Apparently the Outrigger was damaged in the events surrounding the failed Quantum Realignment in that month." Seeing Bolt's disapproving look, he said, "What?"

"Don't you have a heart?" Bolt said. Even Mentaxa had a tear in her eye after witnessing Do-Kar's and Lur-Tela's final moments. "A moment of silence would be respectful."

"Ketrus's destruction occurred a million years after any of us were born," Ramu answered. "It is an accomplished historical fact. One might just as well observe a moment of silence for the victims of the Trojan War, or the Black Death, or the last days of California."

"It isn't the same," Bolt said. "If you don't see that, then I feel sorry for you."

"I do not require your sympathy. I require only direction. You have heard me state our options; to which time would you like to travel next?"

Mentaxa said softly, "If we're going to stop Arras Pou-Dinh from changing history, it would help to have powerful allies. I think it's time we met the legendary Ran-Arl...."

❖

The world was in bad shape.

Germany again on the rise, led by a madman. Economic depression throughout the industrial West. Japan invading China, her armies on the move across Asia. The very British Empire poised on the point of dissolution.

Tsar Alexei was glad that Russia's economy was stable, her armies strong, her borders intact, and her colonial partners largely content. Moskva was the city of the future: the subways were clean and bright, dirigible airships from near and far called daily at the tallest buildings in the world, the commerce of half a continent moved through the markets of Moskva.

Still, Russia could not hide behind her borders and her neutrality much longer. War was coming to Europe, to the world, and choice would soon be inevitable.

"We need to act before it is too late." Defense Minister Vlasov was a hothead, eager to test the mighty Russian Army against Germany. "Already Germany looks lustfully toward Austria. Next it will be Czechoslovakia, then the wolf is on our doorstep."

Foreign Minister Kirov shook his head. "Herr Hitler has hinted that he would be in favor of a nonaggression pact."

Alexei grunted. "*That* weasel-eyed fool?! I don't like him, nor do I trust him."

Down the table, Science Minister R. S. Pouttin cleared his throat, and all eyes turned on him. In the few months he'd been part of the Cabinet, Alexei and the other Ministers had learned that he was a man of brilliant ideas and few words. When Pouttin talked, it was time to listen.

"It seems to me," he said slowly, as if still at a blackboard in front of a class of college students, "that we face the danger of a two-front war. There is no doubt that Germany will attack...the only question is when. And Japan will not be content with Manchuria; in time she will surely turn on our Pacific possessions." Pouttin took off his glasses, wiped them, and seated them again on the bridge of his nose. His eyes, magnified, were locked on Alexei's. "At the same time, we cannot afford even one major war, let alone two. Our prosperity would leak away like water into sand."

After a pause, Alexei said, "What do you suggest, then?"

"Ahem. Yes. I don't suppose you are at all familiar with the work being done in our physics labs by Professors Einstein, Bohr, and Oppenheimer?" Without a pause, Pouttin answered his own question, "No, of course not. It's very refined physics, only comprehensible to eggheads, all quite hush-hush." He glanced around the table, as if evaluating the trustworthiness of each Minister before proceeding. "In essence, they are learning how to release the energy of the atom. Oppenheimer tells me that in a year or two we could have a bomb, driven by atomic energy, capable of destroying an entire city on its own."

Vlasov laughed. "An atomic bomb! I think you have been talking to that American, Buck Rogers!"

Pouttin cracked a smile. "It does sound improbable. But I am sure that my team knows what they are talking about." His grin faded. "If there is to be war, let it be war on our terms and when we are ready for it. I propose that we fund a highest-priority project for these physicists to construct atom bombs, secretly. When they are ready, Russia can strike at her leisure. And then," his electric gaze was impossible to resist, "and then, all Europe will be ours, from the Elbe to the Urals. And we must not be too quick to dismiss Herr Hitler, as an ally or a subject. He may prove…quite useful. Gentlemen, this is Russia's destiny."

The next day, Alexei put his seal on an executive order creating what Pouttin called the Kremlin Project.

Destiny….

❖

It was a quiet summer day, and Giles Erey, Jr. had the old swimming hole all to himself. An abandoned quarry, flooded when the CCC put up a dam, the swimming hole was about the most isolated spot within ten miles of town. To get there, you had to climb over three fences and make your way through underbrush as thickly grown as any Amazon jungle. The only easy way to get there was by air. A few more years worth of kids, Giles knew, would beat down paths that even the youngest could follow; but for this golden summer of

1936, only the bravest and most determined boys could make their way here.

Stripped to his shorts, Giles perched on a sun-warmed granite outcropping twenty feet above the deep, still water, letting the warm air dry him off and savoring the unaccustomed tranquility. In his thirteen years, Giles hadn't had many moments of peace. He closed his eyes and unfocused his hearing, letting sound and sensation wash across him without leaving any tracks. For once it was nice to be lazy, doing nothing.

A shadow fell across him, and Giles looked up to see a tall, red-haired girl in the most outlandish costume of turquoise. She grinned at him. "Hello, Power Lad," she said.

Giles felt suddenly cold. She knew! But how?

He forced himself to remain calm. "Huh?"

"You're Power Lad, aren't you?"

"D-don't be silly. I'm not Power Lad. Nobody knows who Power Lad really is."

The girl gave him a conspiratorial look. "You're Giles Erey, Jr., aren't you? A.K.A. Power Lad, A.K.A. Ran-Arl of Ketrus?"

Giles slowly pulled himself to his feet. She was four or five inches taller than him, but in muscle and bulk he had it over her by half again. "Who are you?"

She held out her hand; he pointedly ignored it. "My name is Bolt. I'm part of the PsiScouts. We come…from the future."

Giles forced a chuckle. "Is this some kind of a prank? What is it, is April Fool's Day late this year?"

"Look." The girl called Bolt pointed at a rough outcropping, a two-foot chunk of rock half split off from the quarry wall. Abruptly, there was a flash and a tiny bolt of lightning drew blue-white lines between her fingers and the rock. With a crash, the outcropping broke away and tumbled, landing with a splash. "I'm from a group of psi-powered teenagers five hundred years from now. I know all about your secret alias because in my time, your life is a matter of public record."

"Why are you here?"

She frowned. "Because we need your help to save the world."

Giles nodded. "Saving the world I can deal with. Look, I feel somewhat exposed here. Would you mind if we went somewhere else to talk?"

"Good idea. Where did you have in mind?"

"How about my parents' house? I can take you there."

"That's all right," Bolt said with a mysterious smile, "we know where it is. First, let me introduce you to the others."

❖

Coulomb had witnessed the scene a thousand times, in every interpretation from animated cartoons to high opera, but still he felt a thrill as Giles, moving so quickly that he was only a blur, donned the famous red-and-blue suit with its gaudy chest insignia and absurd billowing cape. Then Giles leaped, and flew away to the south before Coulomb could gather his wits.

Bolt folded her arms across her chest and nodded. "All things considered, he's taking this well." Then she stepped into the radius of the temporal bubble and said to Ramu, "Let's go. Can you get us there just before he arrives?"

"I am setting the time displacement for minus three minutes. That will suffice."

The time trip took only an instant; reality blinked, and Coulomb was standing with the others in a darkened basement, rough timbers overhead and bare concrete walls all around.

A wood-planked trapdoor set into the cement floor lifted, and Power Lad popped into view. He stopped dead, floating a few centimeters above the floor, and squinted at the PsiScouts. "You're fast, I'll give you that."

Now that he had a moment to look closely, Coulomb saw that there was a definite physical difference between Power

Lad and Giles Erey, Jr. Ketrussi psychokinesis—boosted to incredible strength by the energetic neutrinos spewing out from Earth's hot yellow sun—allowed Ran-Arl to sculpt his face and physique as he moved between the two identities.

As Power Lad he was stocky, firm-muscled and trim, with vaguely elfin features and a obsidian hair with a distinctly midnight blue cast. As Giles, however, he seemed to lose a handful of kilos and gain a few centimeters in height. His complexion darkened, his hair became more of a mahogany shade, and his facial features grew less exotic. Heavy-framed eyeglasses and clearly-unstylish clothes provided the final touch.

"Of course we're fast," Bolt answered. "We have a time machine."

"Five hundred years in the future, eh? So tell me, what's it like? An aeroplane in every garage? Mile-high buildings? Universal peace and brotherhood?"

Bolt snorted. "We wish!"

Ramu Fornix said, "We cannot tell you specifics of the future. To do so would to risk altering our own past."

Power Lad nodded. "I guess I can understand that. What if you told me there was another Great War in twenty years, and I did my best to stop it from happening?" He sighed. "Still, it would be nice to know."

"Or maybe it *wouldn't* be so nice," Mentaxa commented.

Power Lad shook his head. "All right, then, tell me how we're going to save the world."

Bolt, assisted by the others, gave him a thumbnail explanation of Arras Pou-Dinh's raid and the threat he posed. "We have to find him, undo whatever damage he's done, and take him back to our own time," she finished.

Power Lad whistled. "That's not going to be easy. There are a billion people on this planet—how are we going to find *one*?"

"Arras Pou-Dinh may not even be in this time period at all," said Ramu. "Once he has built his own time machine, he will almost certainly skip through time, stopping only to make adjustments at crucial periods."

"Can you determine what those crucial periods *are*? If so, we can use your time machine and be waiting for him at the next one."

Ramu frowned. "I am not as conversant as I should be with the history of Earth's Petroleum Age. Nor does the Aarnal overmind contain the information I need. At best I can guess."

Coulomb put his hand on Ramu's shoulder. "I did a term paper on Petroleum Age politics in sixth grade. Between that and the general databanks from our suit computers, we should be able to make those guesses a little more reliable." He chuckled. "I *hated* that unit. My counselor would be surprised if he could see me now."

"We will need to access your databanks," Ramu said to Power Lad. "How do we sign on to the Net?"

Power Lad looked blank. "Net?"

Coulomb grinned. "He means that we need to take a look at a library. Preferably one with a good history section."

Power Lad looked from one to the other, shook his head, and chuckled. "Not dressed that way, you aren't." He gestured at Ramu. "And I don't think even new clothes would help you avoid attention. Folks around here aren't used to seeing green-and-silver people."

"No, I *must* examine historical records personally," Ramu insisted.

"What if I link Coulomb to you telepathically?" Mentaxa asked. "You'll learn everything he learns, and you can direct him to research anything you need to know."

Ramu nodded. "That is acceptable."

"Okay," Power Lad said. "Come upstairs and meet Mama and Papa. Coulomb, you'll fit into my clothes, and I'm sure we can find something for Mentaxa to wear."

❖

The Pulaski Public Library frightened Coulomb.

To begin with, it was crowded. Too many 'dults, all in funny clothes and all of them—especially the librarians—glaring at these three teeners who had the effrontery to invade the sacred precincts of knowledge.

As if *that* wasn't enough to scare any teener, there wasn't a terminal or datascreen in sight in the whole marble edifice. Instead, there were books, *real* books on paper, hundreds of thousands of them sitting around on shelves, totally unprotected. When he found out that you were allowed to touch them—were, in fact, supposed to take them to a table and paw through them—Coulomb needed Mentaxa's help to keep from hyperventilating.

On all of Taarla, there was a total of five books: one in each of the major museums, and another sheathed in diamond film and on display in the President's office. The mere thought of touching a book, opening it up and riffling the pages, felt like sacrilege.

Power Lad—Giles, Coulomb corrected himself—had no difficulty; he strode right to the history section and began pulling books off the shelves. "What are you looking for?"

"I don't know. Recent history, I guess." Coulomb winced. "D-do you have to be so *rough* with those? Those are *books*, you know."

Giles, balancing a priceless volume in one hand, put the other hand on his hip. "I *know* they're books. How *else* are we supposed to find out what you need to know?" He continued browsing, flipping books open, checking their pages, and then slamming them shut. "This stuff is too old; there's nothing here that was published after the turn of the century."

"Maybe we should ask for help."

Giles waved a hand, dismissing the librarians and all other 'dults in the building. "Them? They won't give us the time of day. Stay here, I want to take a look around." Giles turned his head slowly to the left, his eyes focussed in the near distance. When he'd completed a quarter-turn, he smiled. "There's what we want. Follow me."

As it turned out, this time period's version of news archives was something called a daily newspaper. These papers—they were enormous, the size of a pillowcase or larger and printed on invaluable paper—were bound between stiff covers in periods of six months at a time. The volumes were dusty, the paper tan and brittle, and there was no indexing function available at all. Still, after a while Coulomb found that he was enjoying reading them. This wasn't dry vids and empty words on a screen: this was history come alive, the stories of real people and real lives.

Please keep your attention on the task at hand, Ramu's voice said in his mind, every time he strayed from the national and international news. He would force himself back, only to be distracted again by the story of a widow rescued from a burning house, or a local boy making it big in entertainment.

Hours stretched on. Coulomb worked slowly backward, skimming six months of news at a sitting and then getting up to fetch the next volume. Mentaxa sat next to him, silent, her mind forming a link between Coulomb and Ramu Fornix. And Giles fidgeted, went to the bathroom, explored the building, stared out the window. What do I do, Coulomb thought, if Power Lad decides he's leaving? How would I get back to the house?

Coulomb, please try to keep your attention on our research.

The sun sank, shadows in the reading room lengthened, and Giles became even more restless. Finally, Coulomb closed the 1910 volume and sat back with a sigh. *What do you think?* he thoughtcast to Mentaxa and Ramu.

Arras Pou-Dinh has altered the course of Russian history, Ramu answered. *If you are certain of the dates of the Communist Era...*

I'm sure, I tell you! 1917 to 1990. Count on it. The Cold War was the structuring conflict of the entire last half of the Twentieth Century. I could never forget those dates.

...Then it appears that Arras Pou-Dinh has aborted the entire Communist Revolution. Russia is the leading industrial nation in the world at this time. Given Russia's current technological lead, combined with the emigration of Einstein and Oppenheimer from Germany, I expect that Russia will soon develop the fission bomb.

But that's not right. The United States developed the fission bomb first!

Not in this new version of history.

"Are you guys done, or what?"

Coulomb shook his head. Suddenly, the library seemed a dark and suffocating place. He wanted fresh air. "Yes, we're done. Let's go back to your house."

"Good. Mama ought to have supper ready soon. You've never eaten until you've tasted her chicken and dumplings."

They walked the mile and a half from town to the Erey house. It was early evening, and a summer haze hung over the dirt road bordered by large Victorian homes with expansive yards. Giles quietly led the way, which was just as well, for Coulomb and Mentaxa were deep in mental communication with Bolt and Ramu.

The conflict that you know as World War II has already begun in Europe and Asia, Ramu said. *It will only intensify over the next few years. I predict that Russia will win the war with fission bombs, but only after allowing Germany to devastate England and Japan to bomb the American base in Hawaii.*

I think he's right, Coulomb said.

That doesn't tell us when Arras Pou-Dinh is likely to be around.

Germany will invade Russia in June of 1941. Japan will attack Pearl Harbor in December of that year. Sometime in the spring of 1942, then, Russia will bomb Germany and Japan. We can expect the war to be over by June 1942.

That still doesn't tell us—

Grip, Bolt, Coulomb thought. *In our history, there was a major peace conference at Potsdam, Germany in July 1945. Leaders of England, America, and Russia decided the shape of the postwar world. We believe that the Potsdam conference will occur in summer 1942, and that Arras Pou-Dinh will be there.*

Summer 1942. Six years from now. Are you sure about this?

As sure as we're going to get.

So what do we tell Power Lad? We need him to come along...but we don't want to risk disrupting our own history.

Our history is already disrupted, Ramu thought.

We have an idea, Mentaxa said. *If Giles will co-operate, I think I can give him a post-hypnotic suggestion to forget everything he learns about his future when he returns home. No matter what he might learn, he won't be able to act on his knowledge.*

Are you sure you can do that?

No, I'm not sure. But I've been watching his mind, and I'm getting an idea of how it's put together. All I can do is try.

His brain is still Human, Coulomb offered, *no matter how advanced.*

I said all I can do is try. That's what—oops. Here comes trouble.

"Trouble" was two older boys, probably sixteen or seventeen, approaching with the swaggering waddle of bullies in any century. The lead one, taller and older, had dirty blond hair and pimples; the shorter one was dark-haired, with long arms and hands the size of grapefruits. They were obviously either brothers or cousins.

The leader stood directly in Giles' path and stopped him with an outstretched arm to the chest. "Wait a second, Erey. Where do you think you're goin'?"

"Home," Giles responded, sounding meek.

"Didn't I tell you that this is *our* road? Didn't I tell you to keep off?"

Giles gave a forced chuckle. "Come on, Bert, this is the only way home."

"Hear that, Chuckie? He says this is the only way home." Bert seized a handful of Giles' shirt and drew him closer. "I told you to find another way. I don't like seein' your face around here."

Chuckie giggled. "Maybe if he introduces us to his girlfriend, we could let him pass."

"Now that sounds like a mighty fine idea. Who's your girlfriend, Erey?"

"My name is Iris," Mentaxa said, "and if you have something to say to me, say it to my face."

Bert released Giles and danced backward, spreading his arms. "Ooh, the little lady sounds a mite peeved. What are you going to do, Miss Iris, have your boyfriends beat me up?"

"I don't need anyone's help to deal with the likes of *you*," Mentaxa answered.

"Hear that? The lady doesn't need anyone's help." Bert sneered. "How about if Chuckie and me teach your boyfriends here a lesson? Tough girl like you don't wanna hang around with trash like them anyhow."

"Ignore them," Mentaxa said, taking a step forward. Coulomb moved to follow her and Giles, his face a study in uncertainty, came with them.

Without warning, Bert swung his fist at Giles. It connected, and Giles went down in a sprawling heap. He must have rolled with the punch, Coulomb guessed, or Bert would have broken his hand against tungsten-hard Ketrussi jawbone.

Between Mentaxa and Coulomb there was no discussion, no thought, not even an exchanged glance. Their martial-arts training kicked in instantly, and before the bullies knew what was happening, they both landed in roadside grass, the wind knocked out of them. Coulomb gave Giles a hand and helped him up.

"If you ever again bother Giles or either of us, you'll get worse than that," Mentaxa said to the bullies. Then, taking Giles' arm on one side and Coulomb's on the other, she continued in the direction they'd been walking before they were interrupted. When Coulomb turned to look, a few minutes later, the bullies were gone.

"I can't tell you how much I enjoyed that," Giles said. "Giles Erey has to act meek and mild so no one will guess he's Power Lad—but I've been wanting to thrash those boys since I was a child. Thank you."

"I guess the news will be all over town soon, eh?"

"Oh, I think Bert and Chuckie are going to be quiet about this one. But I'll bet they don't bother me for three months at least."

"It must be hard on you," Coulomb said.

"What, acting meek? Nah, it's actually sorta fun. Like play-acting. And Papa says that it gives me sympathy for all the meek people of the Earth."

"Don't you have any friends?"

"Sure. Plenty of them. Except..." Giles looked away. "*Giles* has friends. But I guess Power Lad doesn't."

Mentaxa squeezed his hand. "He does now."

With sunset against the sky and a cool breeze in their faces, the three friends walked back home hand in hand.

❧

Mama Erey's chicken and dumplings were as delicious as promised, and Coulomb ate more than his share. He felt comfortable with Mama and Papa Erey—they reminded him a little of De' Artveldt, even though they were ancient, white-haired and wrinkled while Colleen was merely old. Mama and Papa accepted the Scouts in the house and at dinner as if they were well-accustomed to visitors from other worlds and other times. After dinner Mentaxa and Coulomb changed back into their PsiScouts outfits; Coulomb was glad to be back in his suit.

Power Lad consented to the post-hypnotic suggestion; Mentaxa implanted it that evening, sitting in wooden chairs in the back yard under a skyful of stars barely dimmed by the lights of the town. When she was sure that the suggestion had taken, they began to talk strategy.

"You think this conference in Potsdam will take place in summer of 1942?" Power Lad asked.

"That is correct." Ramu looked ill-at-ease, and jumped as if he'd been stung when a leaping grasshopper hit his leg. "I cannot make a finer distinction until I examine news reports closer to the time."

"What do you want to do," Bolt asked, "stop halfway and get a newspaper?"

"Stopping to examine newspapers every four point three months is a minimax solution."

Bolt threw up her arms. "Why not? Arras Pou-Dinh might as well have as much of a head start as we can give him. Conquering the world is a hard job. He needs all the time he can get."

"You do not understand the mechanics of time travel. We can make an infinite number of stops along the way; we will still arrive at the instant we designate...no sooner and no later. I guarantee you, Arras Pou-Dinh will have no additional time to prepare."

"You'd better be right about that."

"I am."

"Guys," Coulomb said, "can we get on with this?"

"All right." Bolt stood, and the others followed her lead. They crowded together, Giles looking a little uncertain.

"Aren't you going to change into Power Lad?" Coulomb asked.

"Not while I'm standing in Giles Erey's back yard," he said. "I'll change when we're under way."

"Let's go, then," Bolt ordered.

Ramu looked at Giles. "Where is the best place to purchase newspapers?"

"The paper box in front of Wilson's Drug Store downtown, I guess. That's on Main just half a block up from Lincoln Boulevard."

Ramu nodded and gripped the time bauble, which had appeared as if from nowhere. "Prepare," he warned.

The temporal field established itself in an eyeblink, the swirling colors of time travel playing across its surface like a close-up of an Impressionist painting hung on the side of a lurching elephant.

Ramu stood like a statue, one hand on the time bauble and his eyes fixed as if he actually watched the flowing timestream that they were no longer a part of. After a few seconds—or minutes, who could tell?—he gave a nod and the field dissolved.

Downtown Pulaski, like a museum holo of Small Town USA circa 1930, melted into place around them. The sidewalk was firm, the cool air smelled of leaf mold, and the rising sun painted the eastern sky orange and grey. Wilson's Drug Store, six steps to the left, had not yet opened its doors; a string-wrapped bale of newspapers sat next to the entrance.

Bolt reached for a paper, then pulled back as a multicolor shimmer filled the air before her.

"What the—?"

The shimmer resolved itself into a humanoid figure, an older man in a brown business suit and homberg, a man whose face Coulomb would never forget...Arras Pou-Dinh.

Pou-Dinh raised a weapon toward the PsiScouts. "Did you think that I would not watch the timestream for your arrival? Or that I would not be prepared?" He met Mentaxa's eyes. "I could use *your* abilities, child. I will spare you, if you consent to place yourself under my control."

Mentaxa turned her head away with a snort. "Forget it."

He smiled. "Very noble. Goodbye, then." Pou-Dinh fired, and Coulomb felt his feet go out from beneath him.

❖

Falling, spinning, Coulomb pirouetted through time like a single snowflake caught in a blizzard. Colors swirled around him as he tumbled madly, his stomach lurching and his arms flailing in futile search for support. Everything was in motion, nothing fixed, nothing to hold onto.

Closing his eyes didn't help.

Neither did screaming.

Cou!

Mentaxa? Let it be her, let it be her!

Cou? I can't...hold you.

Where are you?

Calm down. I need you to be quiet.

I'm falling! Help me!

Shut up! Her mental command helped to steady him. Center, he thought. Focus.

All right, I'll be quiet.

That's better. Keep your eyes shut. And your mouth. I'm going to bring you into rapport.

He took a deep breath, and felt calm spreading in his mind like summer breeze across tall grass. Mentaxa was somewhere nearby, within reach if not sight; so was Bolt. Coulomb stretched out his arms and felt the spinning maelstrom steady about him.

Here. His hand was in Bolt's, a ghostly presence as much memory as sensation. Her touch, the shape of her magnetic aura, was a stillpoint in the tumbling cosmos. He kept his eyes closed, unwilling to discover that this handclasp was illusion.

Thanks.

Just hold tight. Mentaxa?

I'm right here, she thoughtcast, and Coulomb felt the touch of her hand as well.

Bolt chuckled. *"When shall we three meet again, in thunder, lightning, or in rain?"*

Coulomb felt Mentaxa's frown. *That isn't funny.*

He couldn't resist asking. *Where are we?*

Not so much "where" as "when," I think, Bolt replied. *Mentaxa, hon, can you reach Ramu?*

Ironic sarcasm dripped from Mentaxa's mind. *Now why didn't I think of that? I sense him nearby...unless it's some twentieth-century clockwork automaton. His mind is difficult to link with. All ones and zeroes.*

Coulomb waited, his mouth dry and his stomach still unsettled. They were lost, adrift in the timestream, and only Ramu Fornix had any chance of getting them to safety. All he could do was to keep from disturbing Mentaxa's attempt to reach him.

Ah. Ramu's mental voice was even more emotionless than his physical one. *I see that you three have survived as well. That is good. Our chances are distinctly improved.*

Where are we? Bolt fairly shouted.

Earth, of course. However, we are out of phase with normal time. Arras Pou-Dinh scrambled the time bauble's base settings. I am attempting to re-initialize the unit. Please be patient.

Where's Power Lad?

I don't know, Mentaxa answered. *Maybe I'm just not familiar enough with his mind to feel his presence.*

The time bauble is reinitialized, Ramu reported. *Unfortunately it will not interface correctly with the Outriggers. I suspect that Pou-Dinh has altered the protocols.*

Are you telling me that we're going to have to materialize at another natural disaster?

Remain calm. Coulomb felt an echo of Ramu's hands moving, disassembling the time bauble and moving deftly over the circuitry within. *There is a fluctuation in the timestream nearby. The unit does not have enough sensitivity for a direct fix, but if I can successfully cross-circuit to beta and reverse the polarity of the neutron flow, it is possible that we will emerge at the time of this fluctuation. Prepare yourselves.*

How? thought Bolt, but it was too late. A soundless flash, a stomach-wrenching lurch, and—daylight broke.

❖

Neil Armstrong spotted his landing site while he was still half a mile above the grey expanse of the Sea of Tranquility. In a field of scattered boulders, the site was flat, white, and clear of everything except lunar dust.

"*Eagle*, you are go for landing." The voice of the flight controller was tinny, with no trace of an accent.

"Roger, understand," Armstrong answered. "Go for landing."

Minutes passed, as the LEM settled on a pillar of flame toward the waiting Moon. Armstrong's hands tightened on the controls, preparing to take over from the computer.

"Seven hundred feet, twenty-one down," droned Aldrin. "Six hundred feet, down at nineteen."

Events were moving quickly, now, and Armstrong barely had time to wonder what it would be like, to be the first Americans on the Moon's surface.

"Five hundred forty feet, down at thirty—down at fifteen."

The LEM was drifting too far from the site. Armstrong took the controls, turned the ship upright, and allowed it to drift horizontally, like a phantom helicopter moving silently above this dry sea.

"Sixty seconds," the flight controller warned. Only a minute's fuel left....

"Forty feet. Down two and one half."

"Come on down, boys. There's vodka and soup waiting for you. Thirty seconds."

"Forward drift?" Armstrong asked.

"Yes," Aldrin said. "Okay."

There was a slight bump, so smooth that Armstrong glanced at the touchdown sensors to make sure.

"Contact light!" Aldrin shouted. Then, calming, he began to run down the checklist., "Engine stop. ACA—out of DETENT."

"Out of DETENT," Armstrong confirmed. They were here. At last, they were here! The landing site was clearly visible out the LEM's windows, as well as the waiting ground crew in hard suits—and beyond them, the faceted domes of Lunograd glittered in the sun.

"Mode Control both Auto. Descent Engine Command Override—Off. Engine Arm—off."

"We copy you down, *Eagle*," the flight controller said.

"Would you mind letting the folks at home know?" Armstrong asked.

"Roger." Houston was monitoring the channel, but protocol demanded that the Russians officially confirm the landing. "Houston, Tsiolkovsky Base here. The *Eagle* has landed."

❖

Two weeks after Apollo 11, Sue Rothjes took off her clothes and went for a walk on the far side of the Moon.

She needed no spacesuit; Sue Rothjes didn't breathe oxygen, and nothing as trifling as hard vacuum and a little ionizing radiation could penetrate her half-Ketrussi hide. All she wore was her action suit, a red-and-blue number that was a virtual copy of her father's famous uniform, down to the stylized "P" on the chest.

Sue Rothjes—she almost never thought of herself by her Ketrussi name, Zun-Kela—kangaroo-hopped across the silent Lunar surface in search of a particular crater. It was such a relief to move around freely, not to worry about disguising her presence from prying eyes. The nearest eyes were at Lunograd, and five thousand kilometers of rock was between her and them.

Her masquerade had lasted all her life, and she was by this time heartily sick of it. But Power Man insisted, and so did his lawyers and his PR flacks: she had to be sixteen before she was permitted to operate openly as Power Maid. Until then, her very existence was secret.

Except on the Moon, where there was nobody to see.

She found the crater she was looking for, and was within its walls in a single bound. There, nestled against the crater rim under a rock overhang that shielded it from satellite cameras, was the tiny survival ship that had carried her father's bio-capsule to Earth.

"Let's see if you're still operational," she muttered soundlessly. At the touch of her finger, a circle of the boat's skin irised open, revealing a padded cargo area, just large enough for an adult Ketrussi, and a rudimentary control panel. Lur-Tela's handiwork was visible in the spot-welds and hand-lettered labels on the console. Sue touched the panel, and a tiny display screen lit with the Ketrussi characters that signified: "Ready."

She crawled inside, let the hatch close her in. It was comfortable and cozy inside the boat; hardly the claustrophobic nightmare she'd expected. Warm air flooded the compartment, making her skin crinkle as it reached Ketrussi pressure. She breathed, and a thousand memories sprang from the forgotten smells of the long-lost world. Since she was ten, Power Man had been giving her periodic memory implants from the crystalline lattices that preserved the last thoughts of Ketrus's scientists.

"Damn it, it's not *fair*." Sue crossed her arms and squeezed, as if she could wrap herself into so tight a ball that she would disappear from the world. She might as well disappear— there was no such person as Sue Rothjes, anyway. Sue Rothjes was a mask, a sham, a living lie with no real life and no real friends. Even the kindly Earth couple who had taken her in, and who now called her daughter...even *they* didn't understand what she was going through.

Nobody understood. And there was no one she could talk to.

Father...the high-and-mighty Power Man, whose life was going just fine before Sue arrived, who had never really wanted a daughter and seemed to be able to do without one just fine, thank you very much...Father was never around, what with saving the world from one menace after another, then dashing off to a distant galaxy whenever he felt like it. And when he *was* around, he didn't listen to her. Power Man didn't listen, he talked, mostly about his own childhood growing up in Indiana, or tricks he'd discovered for using the psi abilities that Earth's energetic sun gave to all Ketrussi, or transparent little moral lessons designed to make her a better Champion....

He'd be happier if she were gone. Everyone would.

Including her.

Then she felt bad for thinking such a thing. When his wife died giving birth to the daughter she longed for, Power Man had tried his best. And when it became obvious that he could not care for a child and the world at the same time, he found the noblest and best foster parents he could. He'd done well by her. It was just...he was so damned *perfect*.

The boat's engine had been powered down ever since it arrived on Earth: Power Man said that the defective warpdrive interfered with interstellar traffic for kiloparsecs around.

She punched the startup sequence, and felt the engines hum to life beneath her.

It would be so simple...just punch the button, dive into warpspace, and emerge across the galaxy. Somewhere different, somewhere she could be herself without having to hide, somewhere Power Man would never find her. Mr. and Mrs. Rothjes would grieve for a while, sure, but they would get over it. By the time Power Man got back from Outer Grubnatz Major or wherever he'd gone, there would be no trace of her trail.

What if the boat wasn't working any longer? Hesitantly, Sue touched the control pads, tapping out a conservative warp jump to take her to Alpha Centauri. If the boat failed, she could fly back under her own power, just a hyperspatial nip and tuck and then five minutes to Earth. If it worked, however, then she could decide whether or not to jump further....

She punched CONFIRM, and the whole boat vibrated. Before her, rough Lunar terrain gave way to inky blackness, a ragged tear in the weave of reality. She poised her hand over the forward thrust control, her stomach knotting. Maybe this wasn't such a good idea.

Before she could slap the control, something moved within the warp. Something metal...something big...and coming this way.

Hastily, Sue slapped the power-down sequence, but it was too late.

◈

Another damn moon, Coulomb thought as existence firmed around them and his suit reacted by sealing him in. Desolate, dusty rockscape stretched away beneath a sable sky, powerful unfiltered sunlight made blinding highlights and inky shadows, and he was too light. Were they back on Ketrus's moon again?

Then Bolt hit him from behind, knocking him to the hard ground just a second before something very large passed above him. Some kind of spaceship, only a meter above the ground and traveling as if chased by demons. Thirty meters away it hit the ground and skidded to a stop in a shower of dust.

"T-That's—"

Bolt looked at him and nodded. "Ut Napis. I think I know where and when we are." She stood up, offered a hand to Mentaxa and Ramu, who were sprawled nearby. "Come on, let's make sure he's okay."

The PsiScouts ran, but something—someone—beat them to Ut's ship: a blue-and-red blur that resolved into a female teener with long blond hair, a gorgeous figure, and no protection from the Lunar vacuum except a tight action suit. She pulled at the crumpled skin of Ut's vessel, tearing hunks of metal loose as if they were tissue paper.

Before she finished, though, another figure emerged from the hole she'd created: Ut Napis, clad in the silvery thermsuit he'd worn when he left Ketrus's moon. Despite the passage of decades, he looked no older than the last time they's seen him.

Bolt held out her arms, stopping the others in their tracks. "This ought to be fun," she whispered.

Power Maid's eyes widened at Ut's appearance. She turned, saw the Scouts, and her mouth dropped open. With an upraised finger, she signaled for them to wait, then retreated to a lifeboat nestled against the crater rim. Rooting inside, she produced a small patch, which she applied to her throat. It clung as if by static electricity.

Coulomb heard a click in his comm unit.

"All right, who are you?" Power Maid demanded.

Ut frowned, wrinkled his brow, then said in accented Galangua, "I...do not...understand."

An instant later, Coulomb's translator repeated Ut's words in Anglich. At the same time, fine print raced across his visual field, asking if he wanted the unit to transmit outgoing voice on this channel into Galangua. He twitched his right pinky, acknowledging the request and giving the go-ahead.

Power Maid was not slowed down. At once, in textbook Galangua, she said: "Who are you? What is your name?" She glared at the PsiScouts. "All of you."

When the most powerful woman in the universe demands your name, Coulomb thought, you don't hesitate. Bolt introduced the Scouts, while Ut sputtered.

Ut is seriously confused, Mentaxa commented. *Probably a side-effect of his long exposure to warpspace.*

Power Maid put her hands on her hips. "Well?"

"I think my name...is Do-San."

Power Maid's eyes widened again. "Do-San?" She looked him up and down. "You're Ketrussi?"

Coulomb opened his mouth, but Bolt's hand gripped his wrist and silenced him. On a private channel, she hissed, "Don't say a word. History tells us that she thought he was Ketrussi. We can't chance altering that. We can't tell either of them who he is until she learns it herself."

Coulomb looked through two layers of transparent suitfabric into Bolt's electric green eyes. "And by that time..." he took a breath. "You mean we're supposed to sit aside and let him be—"

"Hush! Not around them."

Coulomb pulled his wrist free from Bolt's hand. "We have to talk later."

"Bet on it."

Ut was still trying to answer Power Maid's question. "I remember Ketrus," he said slowly. "I...I think I was there once. I know...I know that my name is Do-San. I'm positive of it."

"With a physique like that, you're Ketrussi all right," Power Maid said. "I'm Zun-Kela. We must be...cousins of some kind."

Ut laughed. "You don't look a *thing* like me." He waved at the PsiScouts. "You look more like them."

"That's because I'm part Human. If you're going to stay on Earth, Do-San, you need to know that Humans aren't very tolerant of people who look different." She turned to the Scouts. "So what's *your* story?"

Bolt straightened her back, managing to tower nearly five centimeters over Power Maid. "I'll tell you as much as I can... Sue Rothjes."

"S-Sue Rothjes?" Power Maid's words stumbled over one another. "Th-that's ridiculous. I mean, I don't even know who this Sue Rothjes *is*. I told you, my name is Zun-Kela."

Bolt pushed ahead. "Sue Rothjes, foster daughter of Joe and Nola Rothjes, also known as Zun-Kela, daughter of Ran-Arl of Ketrus, born in 1954 and served a secret apprenticeship under your father, Power Man, until your existence was revealed to the world in—" Bolt stopped herself and chuckled. "But that's the sort of thing I'm not permitted to tell you."

"You'd better let me know what you're talking about...."

"We're from the future," Bolt said. "We came back to...this time period because we need your help." She looked at Ut. "Both of you."

Power Maid's eyes narrowed. "How do I know you're *really* from the future? Who's the current President of the United States?"

That one was easy: Coulomb had seen the man's name a million times on reproductions of the Eagle's commemorative plaque at Tranquility Base. "Richard M. Nixon," he answered confidently.

She laughed. "You're wrong, it's Rockefeller. Nixon is Vice-President." Then she frowned. "You're not telling me that something's going to happen to President Rockefeller?"

"That's part of the problem," Coulomb said. Bolt was watching him intently, and through Mentaxa's residual mental link he felt Bolt's suspicion. "Don't worry, Bolt," he said, "I'm not going to tell her anything she shouldn't know."

"Go on."

"Tell me about Russia," he invited Power Maid. "How powerful are they?"

"The Russian Empire? Only the most powerful nation on Earth. *And* on the Moon. Russia controls the League of Nations, the World Police, the International Armed Forces, and just about every other international organization you can imagine." She shrugged. "Mostly they leave the United States alone. I think they're afraid of Power Man."

"In the future we come from," Coulomb said, picking his words with care, "The Russian Empire started breaking apart before World War I, and was gone without a trace by the early Twenty-First Century. The United States, not Russia, landed the first crew on the Moon. The United Nations, not the League of Nations, settled the Solar System. The Constitution of Earth is based on the Constitution of the United States, not Russia's. And Nixon was President in 1969, not Rockefeller."

"What happened?"

Briefly, Bolt outlined their struggle with Arras Pou-Dinh. Coulomb noticed that she left out any reference to Ut Napis.

"Wow," Power Maid's eyes widened. "You actually visited Power Man when he was young?"

"Yes. We lost him when Pou-Dinh attacked us."

"Not to worry," Ramu said. "Since Power Man exists now, we know that Power Lad made it safely back to his own period. Perhaps we should consult with him. What is his current location?"

"He's in another galaxy," Power Maid answered.

Bolt asked, "What about the League of Champions?"

"I'm not supposed to reveal myself to them," Power Maid said. "Only Nightrider." She smiled. "Besides, we don't need them. Look, you've got two Ketrussi at your disposal, plus your own abilities—what could we possibly run into that we can't handle?"

"Overconfidence—" Ramu began, but Power Maid cut him off. "Look," she said, moving toward Ut's crumpled ship, "if we're going to have a long debate, let's go somewhere a little more private. Get inside, and I'll take you there." She tucked her fingers under the ship and lifted; it rose gracefully, dripping Lunar dust.

Bolt shrugged and walked to the now-useless hatch. Coulomb and the others followed.

Power Maid snagged Ut by the forearm. "Not you, Cousin. You stay with me. The neutrinos from Earth's sun boost all of your psionic powers—you'll have to learn how to handle yourself. This is your first lesson."

❖

In 1969, the Sahara Jungle was a bleak and sandy desert, dry and oven-hot beneath a merciless sun. Power Maid and Do-San, flying low over the endless dunes, carried the wreckage of Do-San's ship to a ten-meter-tall cairn of weathered stones, the only landmark in sight. Hovering above it, Power Maid concentrated; in a moment, a twenty-meter circle of desert floor sank, revealing a gaping pit. As they settled downward, Do-San's ship cleared the edges with meters to spare.

The walls of the shaft were sheer, with no sign of a stairway, ladder, or even handholds. For perhaps half a kilometer they settled, then the ship lurched as Power Maid and Do-San set it down on a rocky floor. Exiting, Coulomb felt cool, moist air on his face and hands.

"Welcome to the Stronghold," Power Maid said, still speaking in Galangua. "Power Man built it, I added to it. Nobody knows it's here, and nobody can listen to us."

Mentaxa looked around at bare stone walls, garish artificial light, and awkward-looking metal support beams. "Lovely," she said.

"The living areas are this way." A portion of the stone wall dissolved into an archway, and Power Maid led them into a vaulted chamber whose muted earth-tones and sturdy, overbuilt furniture recalled Do-Kar's apartments on Ketrus's moon. "Please make yourselves comfortable. I'll be right back."

Do-San pulled off his thermsuit, leaving him in the red-and-black Ketrussi jumpsuit that he'd borrowed from Do-Kar and Lur-Tela. He stared at Bolt, then shifted his gaze to Mentaxa, Coulomb, and Ramu. His brow creased, he said, "Have we met before? I feel that you are familiar, but I don't know who you are."

Bolt said, "I'm sure you would remember if we *had* met."

He waved, indicating the Stronghold, the desert, the entire planet. "This is all so new. Zun-Kela, and these powers. And this world. I'm so confused."

Power Maid returned, carrying a set of bulky headphones. She held them out to Do-San. "This is a Ketrussi educator. It'll adjust itself to your brainpattern, then will give you English, Russian, and enough about Earth history and society to let you get around safely. It'll take about a half hour."

Do-San took the educator and settled it on his head. His eyes became glassy, and he settled slowly back in his chair, to all appearances completely relaxed.

"While he's learning," Power Maid said, "we can decide what to do about your problem."

Ramu cleared his throat. "I see that Power Man maintains an Aarnal-designed computer tied into Earth's major communications channels."

"That's right. But how did you know?"

"I, myself, am an Aarnal-designed computer. I have accessed your system and reviewed geopolitical events of the last fifty years. Your history is diverging from ours at an increasing rate. This limits my ability to make useful predictions. However, it seems likely that Arras Pou-Dinh will appear at the OPEC oil cartel summit meeting in November of this year. If we are to continue with our plan of confronting and stopping him, that place and time gives the best probability of finding him."

"How likely is it?" Bolt asked.

"I compute a probability of 83 percent that he will be there. The probability that we will succeed in thwarting his plans is incomputable."

"We have four months to come up with a surefire way." Bolt turned to Power Maid. "What do you think?"

"I think we ought to fly out to Moscow and scan the place with clairvoyant vision to find this guy." She smiled. "But Power Man's always telling me I'm too impulsive, and that I should take time to plan before I act."

"Oh, yeah," Coulomb said, "we *always* do that."

Ramu shook his head. "Pou-Dinh is probably out of the timestream at this moment. You will not find him in Moscow or anywhere else."

"Well, we can't do anything until Do-San is finished," Power Maid said with a sigh. "Why don't you all wander around, explore the place. You can't hurt anything; all the really vital areas are sealed off."

"I'm hungry," Coulomb said.

"I'll show you where to get refreshments."

◆

Power Man's Stronghold, packed with Ketrussi technology and conveniences, was like a little island of the future in Twentieth-Century Earth's sea of primitive simplicity. Chamber Eight, the viewing room, was ringed with hundreds of data screens carrying news and entertainment broadcasts from all over the planet—and a few alien cultures as well. Coulomb sat down in a comfortable chair at the center of that ring, and marveled at the brainpower necessary to attend even a tenth of the display.

Bolt circled in front of him, touched her suit's privacy code. Her words, oddly distorted by the dampening field, reached him as if from kilometers away. "You don't agree with me about Do-San."

He straightened his back. "No, I don't."

Bolt was obviously keeping her anger in check. "All right, what do you think we should do? Tell them both what's going to happen?"

"He deserves to know."

"Does he? At the risk of rewriting our history?"

Coulomb looked away. "I don't care what Ramu says. I don't care what anybody says. He should know."

"Suppose it was you?" Coulomb whipped his head around to look at her. "No, I'm serious. Suppose *you* were the one poisoned by ultraviolet light? Suppose I told you that your proteins are disintegrating, all your tissues are going to fall apart, and you've got less than six months to live? That those six months are going to be agonizing, and the damage is already done and there's nothing anyone can do for you? That if you leave Earth and return to Ixtal right away, maybe you can stretch it out for a year, but you're still going to die?"

"He *didn't* die," Coulomb protested.

"No," Bolt agreed, "he didn't. Because *she* put him into the Shadow Domain, where he couldn't die. Or age. And it broke her heart, according to the story." Her lips tightened. "But if you want to tell them, be my guest." She stepped back and waved toward the door. "Go right ahead. Tell him that he's got six months of pain followed by eternity of sensory deprivation. Tell her how soon she's going to lose the big brother she just found. I'll wait right here."

"I...I don't know what to do."

"Royd, your heart's in the right place. It just needs to catch up with your head." She reached over and playfully chucked his chin. "Stay here and think about it. I know you'll make the right decision."

Bolt departed, leaving Coulomb alone while the world played out around him.

❖

Chamber Six was a solidographic re-creation of the outpost where the Ketrussi scientists had lived in those last days, complete with claustrophobic passageways, ruddy sunlight streaming through windows, and the smell of too many people living without hope for far too long.

Power Maid came here when she wanted to be alone; Power Man understood, and never interrupted her when she was in Chamber Six. Sometimes she called up holos of the people whose memories she carried...but that was when she *really* wanted to wallow in self-pity.

Today, she stood in the agri-dome, where a few species of Ketrussi trees and flowers—those which escaped destruction in the wars—had grown in artificial soil and chemical compost. To the younger scientists, who had never known life before the devastation, this garden had seemed lush beyond imagination; only the elders knew that it was only the dimmest reflection of the lost jungles and fields of Ketrus.

And now, even that reflection was gone. She was left with this copy of a reflection, reconstructed from holos and her own memories, themselves a copy, doubtless flawed in a million ways that no one would ever know.

She heard a noise behind her, turned to see the girl who called herself Mentaxa. She was pale and fragile, this girl from the future, a porcelain doll in black and white. Yet Power Maid couldn't help being impressed by her indifference and obvious disdain for the universe in general. In the vernacular, the subtleties of which Sue Rothjes was still trying to master, Mentaxa was "cool."

"Am I to take it, then," Mentaxa said, leaning against a gnarled tree trunk, "that you've decided *not* to run away? At least for now?"

"Wh-what are you talking about?"

"Oh, please. I thought you were smarter than that. I'm a mind-reader, remember? And you've been broadcasting since we met." She ran her hand over the trunk. "Very nice. Convincing. Much better than a standard VR set in my time."

"I wasn't going to run away."

"No?"

"I just wanted to have some time to think. I started up the survival ship because I was curious if it still worked."

Mentaxa looked upward, past spreading limbs and into star-flecked space. "It must be very difficult, keeping your secret."

"I manage."

"If it were Bolt, now, she'd be going crazy without any friends that she could talk to. I think Bolt would be just about crazed with loneliness." She lowered her gaze. "But you and me, we're different. We don't let it bother us. Who cares about all the rest of them, anyway? You and I know we're better than they are."

Power Maid shook her head. "I didn't say—"

"I have to confess to you, Kela, I for one am glad we came back in time. I'm glad to have the chance to meet you and talk with you like this. See, I grew up being different. Everyone on Ceres is a telepath, but my Talent is so much stronger than theirs...I knew what they were all thinking. And like you, I had to hide my abilities, else the other kids would have torn me apart. I never knew Father...I was a contract deal...and Mother died in childbirth when my little sister developed empathic spasms."

"I'm sorry."

"That's why I'm glad I got to meet you. You *understand*. It makes a big difference, to have a friend who knows what I'm talking about."

Power Maid opened her mouth, then closed it. For a long while she stared out the port, and when she turned her face back, Mentaxa saw tears on her cheeks. "I know what you're saying. It...is hard to live without friends. And I'm also glad that you came to my time. Very glad."

"Good." Mentaxa gave a short, positive nod. "And once we get this mess straightened out, you'll come to our time, where you can be yourself without having to worry."

"Great."

"What time is it?" Mentaxa asked, even though her suit was able to give her the time on two hundred worlds at a simple command.

"About time for Do-San to be done his education," Power Maid said. "Come on, let's go see."

"I'll call the others."

❖

Do-San was more confident and less confused. His spoken English emerged with an accent that Power Maid said was vaguely Hindu, although to Coulomb it sounded just like Standard English. The PsiScouts brought him up to date concerning Arras Pou-Dinh and Ramu's suggestion for the next time to find him.

Do-San frowned. "You said that Pou-Dinh was ready for you last time. What makes you think he won't do the same thing this time?"

"Because," Bolt said, "we're not going to use the time machine. It's only four months, we can wait that out. Ramu thinks Pou-Dinh can detect us entering the timestream, and that's how he homed in on us before."

"Then," Do San said, "we should find out where this international conference is being held. We ought to visit the site, familiarize ourselves with it, and make plans. If you are right, we will only have one chance to stop Pou-Dinh."

"What can he do to us?" Power Maid said. "We have a mind-reader, two Ketrussi, plus magnetic and electrical powers. And a computer-brain to outsmart the guy. We can't lose!"

"Your enthusiasm is misplaced," Ramu said. "With a time machine at his disposal, Pou-Dinh could be invisibly listening to us at this moment. He can visit possible futures and determine how to prevent them from occurring. If he desires, he can ambush any of us when we are least prepared."

"Let him ambush all he wants, what's he going to do to Do-San and me? *Atom bombs* can't hurt us. I've flown through the Sun without even getting a tan."

"According to Power Man's computer records, the probability approaches certainty that the Czar...and therefore Pou-Dinh...has a small stockpile of the substance popularly called 'Ketrussium.'"

Power Maid, very slightly but distinctly, paled.

"What is Ketrussium?" Do-San asked.

Power Maid shuddered, and Coulomb said, "When Ketrus was destroyed, the dying thoughts and feelings of billions of Ketrussi were psychically impressed on the matter of the planet. Chunks were scattered by the Hypernova; quite a number of them fell through the spacewarp that the survival ship opened between Ketrus and twentieth century Earth."

"Power Man has some of the stuff in protected storage here," Power Maid said. "He made me experience it once. It makes Humans uncomfortable, some of them get sick to their stomachs—but for our people it's like crystallized death. I can't describe the pain. Father is sure that a long enough exposure would kill one of us."

"Be assured of that," Ramu said. "Our history has examples."

"All right, then," Power Maid replied, "maybe we *should* take a look at the conference site. And maybe make some plans."

Mentaxa smiled brightly and tilted her head in an obviously-fake parody of enthusiasm. "Or, I know what, kiddos! Why don't we talk the problem to death some more? It's sooo much fun."

Bolt looked down at her. "You've made your point. Ramu, where is this conference going to take place?"

"In the city Riyadh in the Arabian province of the Russian Empire."

"Can you two take us there?" Bolt asked Power Maid and Do-San.

"Sure. San, you take the boys and I'll carry the girls. Follow me."

Before he knew what was happening, Coulomb felt Do-San's iron grip under his arms, and he was airborne. Carrying Coulomb and Ramu as casually as one would carry two sacks of feathers, Do-San followed Power Maid out the door and up the deep shaft that led to the surface. In an instant, they emerged into desert heat so tangible that it felt like slamming into a wall. Another instant, and the Stronghold was lost to sight behind them.

Coulomb's suit stiffened against the impossible wind, and his force screen glowed a dull red as it radiated away the heat of air friction. Ahead, Power Maid and her passengers shone dimly against a darkening sky, racing nightward like a runaway meteor.

His communit beeped, and Bolt said, "P.M. wants to set down in the hills south of the city. She says to tell Do-San to close in and follow closely."

"I'll tell him." Coulomb tapped Do-San on the shoulder and shouted the message. Do-San nodded, and at once they were only meters from Power Maid. The sun slipped beneath the curve of the horizon behind them, and dark came with the swiftness of an electric light going off. Behind and to the left, Coulomb saw city lights and weakly felt twirling magnetic fields; ahead and below, the world was coal black.

Power Maid dived. Do-San called, "We're landing!" and then followed her. Then there was ground beneath Coulomb's feet again, and his suit relaxed. The whoosh in his ears was palpable in its absence, as if it were an old chair suddenly missing from its accustomed spot.

Mentaxa brushed at her hair. "You might have warned us," she said to Power Maid.

Power Maid grinned. "Then you'd have worried. It's like diving into a pool—you have to just close your eyes and jump."

"*You* do, maybe. I'm a one-toe-at-a-time girl, myself."

Coulomb looked around, his suit very gently amplifying the light from a sky so densely strewn with stars that they seemed to overlap. Power Maid had brought them to rest at the bottom of a dry gully, where sand and rock revealed that water had once been here. Now, though, dry air and parched dusty soil showed no trace of whatever torrent had cut the channel.

"Freeze!"

The command came from over the rise to Coulomb's left, and it was impossible to disobey. He felt his muscles lock, saw the others become statues as well.

Arras Pou-Dinh, swathed in flowing robes and holding aloft his green-glowing pendant, stepped over the rise and spat on the ground. "I have always despised children," he growled, "but you whelps raise me to the highest plateaus of hatred." He surveyed them, his eyes like deep desert wells that lacked even the memory of water. "Ah, Power Maid and the legendary Do-San. I have to admit that you *do* keep distinguished company."

Power Maid, struggling motionlessly, groaned.

"Do not try to speak, my dear. Not even the vaunted Ketrussi psyche can resist my hypnotic power." He shook his head. "What a pity to waste such potential. But I cannot permit you to keep dogging my steps across the centuries, interfering with my plans. I shall treat you as all bothersome pests should be treated: with extermination."

A chill ran down Coulomb's back. Suppose Pou-Dinh left them this way, unable to move? In desert sun they might last a day, maybe two or three—but the time would certainly be unpleasant. Of he could simply command them to die. Could Ketrussi think themselves dead? He knew Humans could....

"You: Mentaxa. Step forward." She did so, moving jerkily. "I need your telepathic ability. I want you to mentally command Power Maid to die."

Coulomb trembled but could not close his eyes or turn his head. This is it, he thought. Mama, Daddy, little Bren...I'm sorry. He had never even said a proper goodbye to them. And worse than that, he was leaving them to be born into a universe dominated by Arras Pou-Dinh. His Daddy, more than once, had called him a failure...had any child ever so grievously failed his parents?

Mentaxa quivered, resisting, and Pou-Dinh held the emerald pendant higher. "Follow my orders," he hissed.

Suddenly there was a red-and-blue blur behind Pou-Dinh, shining brightly in Coulomb's enhanced vision. Pou-Dinh spun, his pendant arcing off into the desert night—and with it, Coulomb felt his own paralysis begin to fade.

The blur resolved itself, just for an instant, into the speeding form of Power Lad, twirling Pou-Dinh around like a fish caught in a whirlpool.

"Do not let him reach—" Ramu started to cry...but it was too late, and Pou-Dinh vanished with a subdued "pop."

Power Lad snarled, "I was *that* close to having him. He was in my fingers." He stopped, floating ten centimeters above the ground, and smiled at Power Maid. "Hel-LO. Whose little girl are you?"

Do-San moved as if to put himself between Power Lad and Power Maid, but Mentaxa pushed past him and jabbed her finger into Power Lad's chest. "She's your...er...cousin from the future, and you're going to forget all about her when you return to your own time. So don't get any ideas."

Power Lad looked the way a Human looked when punched—hard—in the stomach. "My...cousin?"

Bolt shouldered forward. "We'll talk about that later. The last time we saw you we were in Pulaski thirty years ago. What happened?"

"And how did you arrive here and now?" Ramu demanded.

Power Lad shrugged. "Pou-Dinh...I assume that was the guy you're chasing, right?" Bolt nodded. "Well, he zapped us with that gun and sent us into some kind of limbo. After a few minutes I got my bearings, but I don't know *what* happened to you guys. I couldn't find you anywhere."

"That does not explain why you are not still lost outside the timestream."

Power Lad managed to look both humble and embarrassed. "Uh...I guess...." He sighed. "I guess Ketrussi can travel through time naturally."

"What?!"

"It must be some kind of psychic power that I didn't know I had. It didn't kick in until I really needed it."

Bolt shook her head. "Wait a minute. You're telling us that you just...flew through time and found us at exactly the right second?"

"No. I've been looking for you for days."

Ramu's face was a study in emotion, as he tried—and failed—to look confused, surprised, and superior all at once. "How did you navigate outside the timestream? What reference points were you able to interface? What did you use as a temporal locus?"

Power Lad laughed. "I don't know. I wanted to find you guys. And I did. I've been following you from Africa. I decided to hang back to see what was going on. Good thing I did."

Bolt looked around cautiously. "We'd better get out of here. Pou-Dinh is bound to show up again."

"We can't go on to Riyadh. He'll be ready for us."

"He'll be ready for us no matter *where* we go." Power Maid sounded on the edge of panic. "How the hell are we supposed to—"

"It's all right, Kela," Do-San said.

At the same time, Ramu singlemindedly continued questioning Power Lad. "You went to no other time periods besides 1930's Pulaski and here?"

Power Lad grinned. "You've got me there. I did a little exploring, sure. I went back to dinosaur times. I actually wrestled with a Tyrannosaurus. You can't believe how big those guys were. Then I watched them building the Pyramids. That got stale pretty quickly."

Bolt coughed. "P.M.'s right. Ramu, forget time travel for a minute and give me your best guess of where we can go to hide from Pou-Dinh."

The greenskinned boy showed no sign that he'd heard her. "You were actually in the Late Cretaceous?"

"Sure, I said so, didn't I?"

Bolt sparked. "Ramu..."

Ramu turned to her. "Do you not understand? Power Lad has demonstrated a psi ability that must be latent in all Ixtal-descended races, catalyzed by energetic Solar neutrinos: an ability to travel in time without disorientation and without temporal locus signatures."

Mentaxa yawned. "Same thing again, Brainboy, but words of one syllable or less this time."

Speaking slowly and distinctly, as if to a rebellious child, Ramu said, "He...doesn't...need...the...outrigger."

Suddenly, Coulomb realized what he meant. "That's right! If Power Lad really was in dinosaur times—"

"I *said* I was."

"—Then he can go anywhere in time. He's not limited to the range of the outrigger."

"And Pou-Dinh *is*." Bolt's eyes lit up as she got it. "P.L. can take us into the past before the Tunguska event. Before Pou-Dinh showed up." She took a breath. *"We can be waiting for him when he arrives."*

"But we *weren't*," Mentaxa said. "Waiting for him, I mean."

"Not in this timeline," Ramu said. "In our original timeline, Pou-Dinh never went back, the Russian Empire fell, and history proceeded in the manner familiar to us. Then Pou-Dinh created a new timeline, in which we now find ourselves. In effect, we will merely create a third timeline."

"Isn't that changing the past?" Coulomb said, his eyes on Bolt.

"No," she answered. *"Repairing* it. Making it what it was supposed to be."

"Stop it," Power Maid said, "you're making my head hurt."

Do-San tried working it out on his fingers. "If we stop Pou-Dinh before he changes history...then there will be no need for the four of you to come back in time to stop him...so you won't, and he'll succeed...so you'll have to come back again...."

"You are making a simple thing complicated," Ramu said. "When I am programming and I delete a line of code, the program does not remember that code was once there. But the logical structure reflects its existence."

"Huh?"

Mentaxa patted Ramu's head. "Let me try. I see where you're going." She thought for a second. "When a painter decides to change a painting, she paints over the old lines. They don't go away, they're always there...you just can't see them. I think that's what Ramu's saying about the universe."

"I thought that was what I *did* say."

"Suppose we *do* stop him, and the world changes back to the way you say it's supposed to be?" Power Maid shivered. "What will *we* remember? The new history, or the old?"

Ramu started to reply, stopped, and thought. Then he said, "Since you will be with us before the point of divergence, I would assume that your current memories will continue to exist."

"Then what happens when we return to our own time? I don't want to be the only one remembering a different history."

Power Lad chuckled at his cousin's words. "My history marks are already bad enough. I can't afford to drop another grade level."

Bolt frowned. "Maybe we ought to try a different plan. The more we talk about this, the creepier it gets."

Ramu crossed his arms. "You are becoming agitated about a non-problem. Returned to your own times, your memories will adjust themselves to the new timeline. Perhaps there will be a period of confusion, but it will pass quickly. Soon, you will never know that there was ever an alternate history."

Power Maid looked at Mentaxa. "I don't want to forget you, either."

Mentaxa swallowed. "I...I think I can take care of that. The same kind of posthypnotic suggestion I gave P.L. should allow you to keep your memories of us and what's happened these last few days." Her brow wrinkled. "It may seem a little unreal, like a dream...."

"There's an old word," Coulomb said. "When a painter changed her picture, sometimes the new paint faded and you could see a ghosted image of the older strokes. When that happened, they called it pentimento."

"That's it exactly," Mentaxa agreed. "You'll retain your current memories as a pentimento."

Power Maid smiled, nodded. "I can live with that."

Bolt raised a hand. "Let's go someplace safe to do this. P.L., can you teach P.M. and Do-San that time-travel trick of yours?"

"I don't know if I can describe it. It's just...something you do."

Bolt looked at Mentaxa, who dipped her head in agreement.

"Semantic memory," she said. "Right-brain stuff. Non-verbal. I can transfer the knowledge."

Bolt tapped her foot in mock impatience. "Would you mind doing so?"

"Da, boss, right away. P.L., relax."

It took less time than Coulomb expected. Mentaxa closed her eyes, took a breath, then moved her hands slightly from Power Lad toward Power Maid, once again toward Do-San. She exhaled deeply. "There."

"Fine," Bolt said. "Let's get out of the time regions that Pou-Dinh can observe.

"Dinosaur times again," Power Lad said. "How about an even two hundred million years ago, right on this spot?"

"Suits me, " Power Maid responded.

Power Maid held out her hands. "Come on, girls! I'll bet we can beat them."

Mentaxa and Bolt took her hands, and the threesome was airborne at once. Coulomb wasn't sure what happened—they just vanished, as if all three had suddenly become invisible.

Power Lad slipped an arm across Coulomb's back and under his shoulder. "Ready?" he asked.

"Ready."

"Last one there's a rotten egg!" Power Lad leapt skyward, carrying Coulomb...then the night dissolved into spiraling fiery rainbows.

❖

The Jurassic jungle was hot and humid, and it stank. The heat and humidity were no problem; Coulomb's suit kept him comfortable. But there was no escaping the odor—which seemed composed of equal parts of rotting vegetables, decaying meat, and dung. He shuddered to think about what might be hiding in the shadows around them.

Bolt, oblivious to the smell and the lurking lizards, drew on the soft ground with a stick. "We know that the Tunguska event occurred...?" She glanced at Ramu.

"30 June 1908, at 7:17 AM local time," Ramu supplied.

"Pou-Dinh appeared roughly six hours before that, or a little after 1:00 AM. He would have started moving immediately in order to be out of range of the explosion. I suggest that we get there about ten the previous night and wait for him to show up."

"Do you know exactly *where* he'll materialize?" Do-San asked.

"Ramu?"

"At ground zero, plus or minus five hundred meters. Well within the range of Ketrussi clairvoyant vision."

"And how do we know where ground zero is?" Power Maid asked.

Ramu cocked his head. "Why, by sending an observer to the moment of impact."

Power Lad nodded. "I'll go. I'll get a good look at the site, and then Mentaxa can transfer it to P.M. and Do-San." He sprang skyward and disappeared. A second later he swooped down through the trees and made a tiptoe landing worthy of a ballet dancer. "Wow, what a blast. The trees were flattened for miles."

"Any sign of Pou-Dinh?"

"I didn't look."

"All right. Mentaxa, do your stuff."

It took only a heartbeat for Mentaxa to pluck the mental image from Power Lad's mind and transfer it to the others.

Bolt went back to her diagram, which bore no resemblance to anything she said. Oh, well, Coulomb thought, at least it made *her* happy.

"P.M., you take Mentaxa and me; P.L., you'll carry Coulomb and Ramu. Circle above the area and we'll pick out a spot to light as near as we can to ground zero. From then on, I want one of the two of you in the air at all times, scanning for Pou-Dinh. Mentaxa, you keep your mental feelers out, and Cou, I want you to feel for any magnetic disturbance. Ramu, watch the bauble in case it gives any warning that Pou-Dinh's arriving."

"And what about me?" Do-San asked.

"You're our secret weapon. Pick a cloud and hide behind it, but keep a clairvoyant watch on us. If Pou-Dinh manages to overpower all of us, then you're the last hope."

"What should I do?"

"Throw rocks at him." Ramu said. At Bolt's surprised look, he continued, "I am serious. A long-distance assault may succeed where a face-to-face confrontation would not. Aim for the head and try to knock him unconscious."

"That's our goal," Bolt said, adding a few squiggles to her diagram. "Knock him unconscious so we can transport him back to 2574." She looked at Mentaxa. "I don't want anyone using deadly force."

"Me?"

"Anyone. Now, he's going to try to use his hypnosis on us, so we have to act the instant he arrives. Coulomb, is there any chance you can snatch that pendant away from him?"

Coulomb thought back to the magnetic signatures he'd sensed when Pou-Dinh was near, and shook his head. "It's gold...non-magnetic." He brightened. "But the time-bauble has magnetic material in it. I can try to get *it* away from him."

"Good idea. P.L., P.M., you're our best bets. Move at hyper-speed, and he won't even see you coming." Bolt moved her gaze from one to the next around the circle. "Everybody okay with this?"

"As okay as we're going to get," Power Maid answered.

Bolt took a breath. "All right, let's get started."

❖

Even in June, the Siberian night was cold. Coulomb stood looking up at stars so painfully bright that he might as well be in space, and watched his breath come out in clouds of white. Gentle ripples of magnetic flux extended in all directions, gradually curving away to the north and south like a silk handkerchief wafting in the mildest summer breeze. There was little here to disturb them, whether man-made structures or buried ore deposits. Detecting Pou-Dinh's arrival would be no problem—this night was so calm that Coulomb was sure he could feel the metal shoes, bits, and buckles of every horse and rider for five hundred kilometers around.

It was way past midnight; just how far past, Coulomb didn't know and he'd suppressed his suit's clock readout. Easier to stay at full alertness, when he didn't know. When Pou-Dinh could appear any second.

Mentaxa had put them all in a first-level telepathic rapport, so that if he thought about it Coulomb was conscious of the others, felt their own vigilance. As silent as a falling leaf, Power Maid landed at the same moment Power Lad took to the sky; the two of them were swapping off on some schedule of their own. High overhead, where the air was thinner and it was colder still, Do-San waited and watched.

Coulomb heard movement behind him, knew from the magnetic signature that it was Ramu. This machine-boy was the most unusual in their whole strange crew, and Coulomb was a little sorry that Ramu seemed so hard to get to know. His face generally betrayed so little emotion, and his voice less, so that it was difficult to know what was going on inside that hardwired brain. And, of course, half of Ramu's thoughts were actually taking place inside the massed computer overmind of Aarnal, kiloparsecs away and five hundred years before his birth. What must Aarnal be thinking of this interloper from the future? Or was time-travel just second nature to the artificial intelligences?

Bolt hissed, a sudden indrawn breath, and Coulomb felt a knot appear in the local magnetic field. Just meters away, almost exactly at the spot Power Lad had identified as Ground Zero.

One-oh-six, Mentaxa thought, glancing at her time readout. *Exactly on schedule.*

"Easy, kids," Bolt said. "Move around him."

Coulomb jumped into position; Mentaxa stood on his right and Ramu on his left, with Bolt and Power Maid completing the circle around the spot. The magnetic knot was now a raging maelstrom...and then Arras Pou-Dinh stepped from its center.

He was facing Power Maid, and before she could move he held up his pendant and barked: "Sleep!"

Power Maid crumpled to the cold ground.

Bolt fired lightning, which coiled around Pou-Dinh without doing any harm. At the same time, Ramu said, "Keep your eyes away from his pendant."

Pou-Dinh turned on Bolt. "Freeze!"

She froze.

In rapport with Mentaxa, Coulomb rolled forward as she leapt. He hit Pou-Dinh's legs and felt Mentaxa slam into the old man's torso, then the three of them were down in a heap. For one splendid moment, Coulomb had Pou-Dinh's arms pinned, and he thought they had won—but in the next instant, rapport snapped like a rubber band and Mentaxa turned on him with fire in her eyes.

Ramu's fist sent her spinning, with a powerful right to the jaw. Then, his own eyes averted, he pulled Coulomb away from Pou-Dinh.

"Thanks!"

"Do not mention it."

"This isn't going well, is it?"

"Listen."

A whistling filled the night, dropping in pitch, and for a crazy second Coulomb thought it was the Tunguska meteor hours early...but it was only Power Lad in a mad dive from above. Coulomb understood why Ramu had pulled him away: Pou-Dinh was a clear target for the Ketrussi .

Until Power Lad halted, only a meter above Pou-Dinh, his eyes closed and his face twisted in agony as he hovered, slowly twisting like a marionette on one string.

"What's wrong?"

Snakelike, Pou-Dinh's bony right arm lashed out and took hold of Power Lad, pulled him closer. "What's the matter, boy? Don't you like my medallion?" He held the pendant to Power Lad's arm, and Power Lad screamed as if it were a hot poker. The boy fell heavily to the ground, and Pou-Dinh pressed the pendant against his chest like a dagger.

Ramu snapped his fingers. "Ketrussium. That's why P.L. and P.M. are so susceptible to his hypnotic power."

"What are we going to do?"

Pou-Dinh turned toward them; Coulomb closed his eyes. "You are going to die," Pou-Dinh said.

With his eyes closed, Coulomb found that Pou-Dinh's command was just words. He kept his attention on Pou-Dinh's magnetic field, backed away as fast as he could. What was he going to do? Pou-Dinh wasn't wearing any magnetic metal, and the native field of his body was too weak to do any damage. There was nothing metal in the vicinity that he could use as a projectile....

Something hit him, hard, on his left side; his suit stiffened, cushioning the impact. At the same time, he heard Pou-Dinh shout, "Kill him, idiot!" There was another blow, but his suit was ready this time. Someone roughly Coulomb's own size was trying to hurt him—but from the feel of the magnetic eddies, much of that person's body was metallic.

Ramu...it had to be Ramu. At once, Coulomb sliced through flux lines with a sharp jab of force; he felt Ramu go tumbling away. He hoped he hadn't hurt the boy.

Power Lad's scream had faded to a pathetic moaning. Mentaxa and Bolt were silent, Power Maid asleep, Ramu down for the count. So far, their moment of glory had not been very successful.

Despite the brilliant stars, it was quite dark—especially for Pou-Dinh, who didn't have a PsiScouts suit boosting his vision. Coulomb ducked behind a tree and circled to the right, while Pou-Dinh was questing in the other direction.

"You're going to wish you were dead, boy," Pou-Dinh shouted. "And so are your friends."

What was he going to do? Visions flashed through Coulomb's mind, visions of snatching the Ketrussium medallion from Power Lad's chest, flashing off through time, and swooping back to stop Pou-Dinh. Visions of creeping behind the old man and knocking him out with a well-aimed chop to the neck. Visions of pulling buried iron ore from a distant mountain and raining it down on Pou-Dinh.

Hell, he might as well have visions of flapping his arms and flying for help.

Damn it, where was Do-San?

...Scared to death, most likely, watching from out-of-range as Power Lad writhed in Ketrussium-induced agony. Afraid to risk it—and why not? What good could Do-San do anyway, if he fell victim to Pou-Dinh?

And the joke—on Bolt, on them all—was that Do-San wasn't even Ketrussi, but Ixtallese. Biologically similar, sure, but if the legends were right, the Ixtallese mind was different enough to be deaf to Ketrussium's psychic projection. During his brief sojourn on Earth, the story said, Do-San had saved

Power Maid from a Ketrussium trap. The stuff should be as harmless to Do-San as it was to Coulomb himself.

No matter. Do-San *believed* himself to be Ketrussi, and that was all that counted now.

He should have told Do-San the truth, no matter what Bolt said.

Cou? Mentaxa's voice was half a whisper in his mind, so faint that he wondered if it was a mere memory. *Don't react. He think's I'm unconscious.* Her presence grew more distinct; he was aware of a slowly-pulsing headache and a throbbing pain in her right shoulder.

Suspicion gripped him by the throat. *How do I know you're not still under his control?*

Like this. Mentaxa opened her mind in the full rapport that was more intimate than any physical gesture could ever be. It lasted only a moment, before her strength faltered and their minds broke apart—but in that moment, Coulomb knew she was telling the truth.

What are we going to do?

Coulomb took a breath. *Can you reach Do-San?*

Probably. What can he do, that P.L. and P.M. couldn't?

Ketrussium can't hurt him.

He doesn't know that.

So you have to tell him. Coulomb heard Pou-Dinh moving in his direction, retreated to another tree as silently as he could.

Tell him...?

Everything. Who he is, where he came from, why he doesn't have to be afraid.

We'll be changing history. Bolt said....

He sent a jolt of anger. *Forget what she said. We're changing history more if we let Pou-Dinh kill Power Lad and Power Maid, and then take over the world.*

She gave a mental nod. *You have a point.*

Let me come along.

All right. Hold on.

Coulomb felt nothing but rough bark beneath his fingers, heard nothing but Pou-Dinh's rustling footsteps. At the same time, he felt as if he were flying, floating above the forest and listening to the endless breath of the wind. Although he saw nothing but enhanced images of trees and ground, he felt Do-San and Mentaxa near him, closer than a breath.

Do-San! This is Mentaxa.

Where are you?

On the ground. In your mind. Coulomb's with me.

What's going on down there? What am I supposed to do?

I'll give you a hint: hanging around the stratosphere isn't doing anybody any good.

He's got Ketrussium. I don't know if—

Coulomb focussed his attention, trying to sound calm. *Do-San, I'm going to tell you something that you're not supposed to know. You've got to believe me.*

Go ahead.

You aren't Ketrussi. You come from the planet Ixtal. Ketrussium can't hurt you.

Do-San was silent for so long that Coulomb feared the telepathic contact was gone. *Do-San? You still there?*

Yes. He sounded dubious. *All right, what should I do?*

Everyone else is out of the fight. Pou-Dinh's getting closer to me. You need to get down here, quick, and knock him out. Before he sees you coming.

Then what?

Mentaxa snorted. *There is no 'then what?' Then it's over.*

You're not just telling me this to get me to—

Pou-Dinh was only ten meters away; Coulomb froze in place and gave a mental shout: *Just get down here, now!*

The mental link dissolved, as suddenly as a comm circuit disconnecting. *Mentaxa? Iris, answer me!* He held his breath, afraid to move, listening. Was there still some lingering awareness of her presence, of consciousness baffled behind layers of cotton?

Pou-Dinh started in Coulomb's direction, and Coulomb forced himself to look away. What now? Run?

The man's eyes, like embers, brushed Coulomb with their gaze. Coulomb tried to turn aside, but it was too late. His arms and legs felt heavy, his eyelids drooped, and all his determination melted away. He was caught in Pou-Dinh's spell.

The last thing he remembered was Pou-Dinh's face, glowing in infrared, lips stretched into a hideous grin of triumph.

Then the world went black.

❖

"Royd, can you hear me? Wake up."

It was his mother's voice. Coulomb struggled through layers of sleep to consciousness. He was in bed, with crisp warm covers tucked around him and the tantalizing smell of warm Taarlan root beer in his nostrils. Stretching lazily, he opened his eyes.

His mother was a solidogram on the comm from home, her half-meter image hanging above his chest. The bed wasn't his at all; he was in a white mediplex room and the bed was monitored a dozen ways from Sunday. Bolt, Do-San, and De' Artveldt stood watching him—beyond them, Mentaxa was in a similar bed with her right arm in a sling.

His mother's image blew him a kiss. "They told me you were okay, but you know how mothers worry. I have to go—take good care of yourself, and do everything the meditrons tell you." She smiled. "We're very proud of you, son. Love you." Then she was gone.

"Wha—?"

"Grip, kid," Bolt said, handing him a steaming mug of root beer. "You're safe. We're back in 2574 and the E.P.'s have Pou-Dinh in custody."

Coulomb looked up at Do-San. "You stopped him after all."

"I nearly didn't. He tried to hypnotize me, but you were right—the Ketrussium didn't affect me."

The shadow of a frown passed over Bolt's face, and Coulomb said quickly, "I had to tell him. There wasn't any other way."

Surprisingly, Bolt nodded. "I know. You didn't tell either P.M. or P.L., and that's the important thing. Do-San has consented to let Mentaxa erase his memory of his origin before he returns to the 1960's."

He doesn't know his fate, Mentaxa thoughtcast. *And we don't intend to tell him.*

No, I guess not. "So finish the story. What happened next?"

Bolt shrugged. "Do-San knocked out Pou-Dinh and took the medallion away from Power Lad. With Pou-Dinh unconscious, his hypnotic influence stopped. P.M. and I woke up, and between us we managed to get Ramu out of the loop your magnetism put him in. After that, it was simple; we bundled up you two, set the time bauble for home...and here we are."

De' Artveldt beamed. "Bolt and the others have told me everything. A fascinating story...absolutely fascinating. I envy you your adventure."

"The others?" Royd echoed. "P.M. and P.L. are here? And where's Ramu?"

"Outside getting interviewed by Jav. P.M. and P.L. wanted to see the future, and I wasn't in much of a position to refuse." Bolt looked from Coulomb to Mentaxa. "If you're feeling up to it, Jav wants to get a few words from each of you. As you can imagine, we're at the top of the nets."

"Of course you are!" De' Artveldt boomed. "Bringing back three living legends from five hundred years ago—the media isn't going to forget this one for a long time."

Interviews. Oh, joy! Mentaxa wore her usual frozen-faced look of general disdain. "All right," she said, "I guess I'm up for it."

"Sure," Coulomb agreed. "Hey, where are Fade and all the rest? Not that I mind the reception committee...."

Bolt cocked her head. "They're at HQ holding down the fort. We'll head over there after Jav gets his soundbytes from us." She held out an arm. Your docs said you can leave whenever you feel like it."

"Thanks." Coulomb let her help him to his feet. He was in the traditional hospital gown, and he wondered who had taken his suit off—the docs, probably. De' Artveldt threw open a closet and handed Coulomb his suit. He moved toward the bathroom. "I'll be right out."

As he donned his suit, the intelligent fabric closed about him, fitting like a second skin, almost as if it were glad to see him again. The suit's computer displayed its ready icon in his lower left visual field, eagerly blinking its report that all system were shipshape and working well.

It took Mentaxa only a few minutes to suit up, then De' Artveldt waved them to the door. As promised, Jav and a crowd of other reporters were waiting outside, and they guided the PsiScouts down the hall to a lounge where Ramu, Power Maid, and Power Lad were waiting.

The joyful reunion—involving many hugs, pats on the back, and broad smiles—was captured on video for the whole Net to see. Jav orchestrated the press conference masterfully, interweaving the Scouts' tale of their adventure with comments about the 2500's from Power Lad, Power Maid, and Do-San.

Eventually Jav announced to the crowd, "Thank you very much, my friends. The PsiScouts have places to be and people to see, and we shouldn't keep them any longer." He turned to a remote, addressing his viewers: "Stay tuned for a special announcement from PsiScouts HQ in a few minutes. This is Jav Emry, signing off."

"What special announcement?" Coulomb whispered to Bolt.

Bolt just grinned. "You'll see."

❖

De' Artveldt refused to sit at the head of the PsiScouts' conference table; instead, she took a seat off to the side. "I'm just a guest," she said, "and honored to be here."

"Colleen, you know you're welcome any time," Bolt said.

Zhene Carmody, as always, was present at the table, and Jav leaned against the wall, devoid of all his remotes and looking uninterested. Besides them, the only ones present were the PsiScouts, arrayed around the table in the informal order that had come about without any real discussion or agreement: Bolt flanked by Coulomb and Mentaxa, Fade and Colossus opposite one another, Mimic and Legion filling out the rest of the circle.

"I call this meeting to order," Bolt said, with a tap of the gavel. "I want to make this short, because Jav and about a billion other people are waiting."

"If we're going to talk membership," Mentaxa said, "then we have to ask Zhene and Jav to leave." She pointedly did not mention De' Artveldt.

"I think we can do this under a privacy curtain," Bolt answered. She thumbed a control, and the dead-air sound of privacy descended. "First off, I want to get rid of this nuisance. I propose that we accept Jav, Zhene, and De' Artveldt as administrative advisors, nonvoting but with all the other benefits of membership under the bylaws. That way we'll be able to drop this curtain, and that we'll get their advice when we need it." She looked around the table. "Any discussion?"

"Go, girl," Fade said.

The motion passed unanimously. Bolt opened the privacy curtain and informed the 'dults of their decision.

"Now for the important matters," Bolt went on. "First, I'd like to propose Ramu Fornix for membership. Discussion?"

"I don't know him well enough," Legion said, "but he seems like a nice guy. A little weird, but aren't we all?"

Coulomb said, "He certainly proved himself with us. His mindlink with Aarnal qualifies as an unusual ability, probably even a psi power."

"If ye vouch, green boy's good enough for me," Fade said.

Colossus shrugged. "Fine with me. Any new blood is good."

"Mimic? Mentaxa?"

"Mimic doesn't know Ramu Fornix. Mimic trusts his friends, though." He blinked. "Yes. Why not?"

Zhene cleared her throat.

"Zhene?"

"There is the matter of his indenture. De' Fornix is attached to the Temporal Institute. I did some discreet checking, and I don't think Dr. Sep-tim-mus would mind releasing him to the PsiScouts. The question is, would *Aarnal* mind?"

"I guess we can only ask. Are there any other comments?" There was no reply. "Let's vote, then. Yeas?" Every hand was raised. "Good. I'll talk to Ramu." She leaned forward on her elbows. "All right, what do we do about P.L., P.M., and Do-San?"

Jav raised a hand and Bolt recognized him. "Bringing them back with you was the hottest public-relations stunt since Orlo Dex explored the Sun. The public loves them. And the public wants them made members, the sooner the better."

"Does the public," Mentaxa asked, "have any idea how difficult it's going to be to hold meetings with three members dead five hundred years?"

"The public doesn't care."

Zhene shook her head. "Dr. Sep-tim-mus is very concerned. The longer they stay in our century, the greater the potential disruption of time. He's particularly concerned about the Ketrussi discovering they can travel through time on their own. What if they decide to use that ability to evade some threat or change the past?"

"What does he suggest we do?"

"The Good Doctor was quite emphatic. He said you should wipe their memories and ship them back to where they belong, the sooner the better."

Mentaxa snorted. "Let *him* try to wipe a Ketrussi's memory without their cooperation."

"I thought you said you gave them a posthypnotic suggestion already," observed Jav.

"That was a temporary measure. I didn't know they were coming into our time with us. The longer they stay, the stronger their memory traces get. You don't know what their minds are like: hard as steel and fast as light."

Bolt spread her hands. "What do we do? I'm open to any suggestions."

Coulomb asked, "What happened to Pou-Dinh's medallion?"

"I guess the cops have it. Why?"

"Well, it's got Ketrussium in it. Pou-Dinh was able to hypnotize P.M. and P.L. without any trouble. I was wondering if maybe Mentaxa could do the same thing. Set up a, whatyacallit, mental block. Reinforce your command to make them forget about the future when they return to their own time."

Mentaxa considered. "Might help. Wouldn't hurt to try."

"What about Do-San?"

For a moment there was silence around the table.

"We have to send him back," Bolt said, sounding defensive. "You saw what happened when Pou-Dinh changed history—we can't do the same thing."

"I didn't say—" Coulomb started, then shut up. Nobody had accused him of saying anything.

Legion's eyes were wide. "Send him back...to die?"

"He's *not* going to die. Power Maid puts him in the Shadow Domain."

"That's just as bad. Isn't there any way we can keep him here?"

Bolt looked around as if for support. "Whether he stays or not, he's already absorbed enough ultraviolet that he's poisoned."

Colossus shook his head and joined the fray. "Our medicine's a lot better than what they had in the 1970's."

"Over a million years, the Ixtalese developed their vulnerability to high ultraviolet. The colonists on Ketrus evolved protection, since Ketrus's sun produced more ultraviolet. Nobody around *here* has the answer to a problem from a million years from now."

Fade snorted. "Shadow Domain ain't so bad, y'know. Pass through on m'way from Earth to home 'n' back." She looked darkly in Legion's direction. "Better than dyin'."

"If he goes back," Zhene said, "Dr. Sep-tim-mus is going to insist that his memory be adjusted."

"Can't do it," Mentaxa said, her jaw set.

"How can you be so sure?" Legion said.

"You've never been inside his mind." She gave an exasperated sigh. "You don't just carve out a section of memory the way you carve a piece of meat. It's more like neurosurgery. You have to follow a lot of tracks to see if they connect to what you want. Then, when you find what you want to remove, you have to untangle the whole track, take it out, and patch any loose ends."

"So?"

"So, his mind resists. Look, removing your memory of last night's dinner is like untangling string. Removing Do-San's memory is like trying to untangle a steel spring. The more you pull, the more it resists."

"Mimic would not try to remove such memories. Mimic would try to *replace* them."

Mentaxa stared at him. "Oh, sure. Just like replacing one stand in a plate of spaghetti, without disturbing any of the others. Look, I appreciate all the suggestions, but I know what I'm talking about and—"

"Couldn't Aarnal help?" Legion said quietly.

Mentaxa stopped in mid-word. "What?"

"The overmind of Aarnal. If you put *it* in telepathic touch with Do-San, do you think it could trace and replace all his memory strands? Or at least help?"

"I...I don't know. It's worth a try, I guess." Mentaxa looked off into the distance. "Yeah, I think that might do it. Provided I have Do-San's permission and co-operation."

"Good," Bolt said. "So you'll ask Ramu about it?"

"Okay."

"And we'll send Do-San back to the past with P.M.?" Bolt looked around the table. "Should we vote?"

Coulomb shook his head. "No need to. I understand that there's nothing we can do to keep him here." He forced his chin up. "But there's no reason we can't plan to get him out of the Shadow Domain someday...."

Bolt nodded. "All right, then. Let's get down to the plaza. We have some new members to induct."

❖

EARTHNET alt.trends.commentary ON Mon May 15, 2574 Sec: 6
Thread: 4
FROM: pjenthen@artveldt.com [PsiScouts PR] AT 17:41:46

PSISCOUTS ADD NEW MEMBERS

New Regular Member:
BioLogic 17 (Ramu Fornix of Aarnal).
Age: 15.
BioLogic 17 is a living computer who can link his mind to the massed computer minds of the planet Aarnal. His vast intelligence and problem-solving abilities will serve the PsiScouts well.

New Honorary Members, on detached duty in the 20th Century:

Do-San (Ut Napis of Ixtal)
Age: 17
A native of the planet Ixtal, Do-San possesses keen clairvoyant senses as well as the powers of flight, heat induction, enormous strength, and near-invulnerability.

Power Lad (Ran-Arl of Ketrus)
Age: 15.
Power Lad, one of the 20th Century's greatest Champions, has numerous psi abilities including flight, clairvoyant senses, pyrokinesis, great strength, and near-invulnerability.

Power Maid (Zun-Kela of Ketrus)
Age: 14.
Power Maid, the greatest Champion of all, shares the psionic abilities of her father, Power Lad.

Following their return to their own century, the three Honorary PsiScouts will remain on call for whenever they are needed most. Their memory of our world will remain buried until triggered to consciousness by a special code phrase implanted by Mentaxa and BioLogic 17.

Citizens of the Myriad Worlds can rest peacefully tonight in the sure and certain knowledge that they are protected by the most powerful group of heroes in history: the PsiScouts.

[Key 298 for coverage of the Scouts' latest amazing adventure.]

Part Two:

*The Case of
the Hunted*

ROLL CALL:
  BioLogic 17
  Colossus
  Fade
  Legion
  Mimic

INTRODUCING:
  Merge

July AD 2574

Legion struggled against the weight bar, his arms quivering as it grew heavier and heavier. His shoulder and arm muscles hurt as if steel bands were tightened impossibly around his body; he was drenched in sweat and couldn't draw enough breath in between teeth so tightly clenched that they were fusing together. His suit had just about given up trying to keep his body temperature in the comfortable range.

Suddenly, it was too much, and he let the bar down into its supports. Gasping, he looked at the readout and felt a surge of pride—three kilos better than his personal benchpress record!

"Not bad." Legion's alter-ego, clad in cool civvies and sipping a box of juice, waved at him from across the gym. "We're getting better every day."

"I thought..." Legion panted, "that you...were supposed to be...studying."

The other lifted his drink in a mock toast. "I'm taking a break."

"That's not the deal." While Legion was here in the gym, another of his six selves was sleeping. One more was in the simulator polishing his piloting skills, and the remaining three were supposed to be in supervised study. When all six merged, most of the benefits remained.

"Teach says we concentrate better with periodic breaks. Besides, how much history can we take at one time? Who cares about the Lunar Revolution anyway?"

"Coulomb says that knowing history saved his butt back in the Twentieth." Incongruous as it might seem to an observer,

Legion was accustomed to arguing with himself. That was how he got all his best thinking done.

"Yeah, well, Coulomb isn't here." The three founding members were away on a six-week publicity tour of the Myriad Worlds.

"But I am," boomed Colossus from the entrance.

"Oops!" Legion-civvies backed away hastily. "Gotta get back to class."

"Wait just a minute," Colossus said, sticking his meter-wide head through the door. "I've spent the whole day chasing one or the other of you back to work. I give up. Do whatever you want."

Legion-weightlifter smiled at his doppleganger. "I want *him* to benchpress for a while." He stood up and moved toward the other.

"Hey, I exercised yesterday."

Colossus reached forward with a hand the size of a large child; Legion-civvies tripped and went sprawling.

"Attention!" The voice was Mimic's, sounding through Legion's communit at the same time it echoed from the gym's speakers. "All Scouts report immediately to the conference room."

"What have we done now?" Legion-civvies asked, as the others raced past him toward the dropshaft.

❖

Colossus beat the two Legions to the conference room...but three other Legions were waiting there when they arrived. Fade and Mimic were already seated at the table, along with Zhene Carmody and Police Chief Ormandeau. A 'dult Human woman in a grey business suit sat with a shy teener girl; the teener wore a dull jumpsuit that shouted "institutional clothing."

Fade frowned. "Took ye long enough. Where Loj?"

"My code name is BioLogic 17, not 'Loj.'" Ramu Fornix, clad in his maroon PsiScouts suit, appeared in the dropshaft. "And I am right here. I hope this meeting will not take long; I left an important experiment in progress." He sat at the table without even a second glance at the visitors.

"Take as long as we need," Fade said. "Ever'body sit down. Legion, too many of ye."

"Right." Legion's six bodies blurred into one. He felt the sudden shock of reintegration, a sensation of nausea and confusion as six sets of memories and six personalities united. The longer his bodies remained apart, the worse the shock when they came together. To cover it, he sat down.

Fade nodded toward the businesswoman. "This Elyene Taurid from Earth Council. Come to ask help. Go ahead, lady."

Elyene Taurid leaned forward, looking uncertainly from side to side. "Ahem. Yes. As...er...Fade has told you, I come from the office of the North American Director of the United Earth Governments. A situation has come to our attention that seems to call for the involvement of the PsiScouts."

Fade cocked her head. "Say what?"

The teener girl met Fade's eyes. "They're killing my friends. You've got to help us." She opened her jumpsuit, revealing jagged scars across her neck and chest. They looked freshly-healed.

Legion gasped at the sight. "Who did that to you?"

"The Hunters. But I got away. My friends are still there."

Elyene Taurid put a protective arm around the girl. "Tammy was spotted in the mountains by a routine infrared wildlife scan; the satellite alerted a regional mediplex and a rescue team was able to save her life."

Colossus waved his hands. "Wait, wait. Start again. Where was this? Who are the Hunters?"

De' Taurid looked gravely from one to the other. "Denver."

Colossus seemed the only one who recognized the name. "Denver? That's—"

De' Taurid nodded. "The Western Capital of the Christian States of America, yes."

"Time out," Fade said, waving her hands. "Start over. Words of one syllable. What ye talking about?"

Zhene sighed. "Don't they teach Earth history any more?"

Fade snorted.

Ignoring her, Zhene continued, "When the Compact was signed, not all of Earth's nations joined the Myriad Worlds. Some of them are still independent today. There's the Muslim Federation, and the Navajo Nation, and Ecuador Freeport... and the Christian States of America."

Colossus punched up a map of North America and waved at a broad swath of color across the center of the continent. "What did you think this was, another ocean?"

Fade shrugged. "Don' know n' don' care."

"You *should* care," De' Taurid said. "The C.S.A. is a nation of religious fanatics who've frozen their society in the middle of the Twenty-First Century. They're as isolated from the real world as if they were on the edge of the Galaxy. And now they're killing children...." She took a breath, then continued more calmly, "Apparently there are a lot of runaways in Denver, too many for the city to handle. Instead of opening their borders and letting the kids leave, the government is organizing hunting parties to go after them. Tammy managed to escape the hunt, even though she was wounded, and collapsed in the mountains just outside the border. It's blind luck that our satellite spotted her infrared trace while she was still alive."

Legion leaned forward. "Why haven't the Earth Police moved in to make them stop?"

Chief Ormandeau spread his hands. "Officially, the C.S.A. is out of our jurisdiction."

"The United Governments and the Myriad Worlds have both tried to intervene," De' Taurid said. "The C.S.A. says that this is an internal matter, and we can't get any further through diplomatic means."

"So you're just letting runaway teeners get shot?"

"Colossus, we've only known about this situation for a week. The government has done everything it can. Now we need you."

Fade looked from one PsiScout to another, as if reading their thoughts. "Go on. What ye want us to do?"

"Send a team into the C.S.A. and put a stop to this brutality."

There was a stunned pause, then Colossus laughed. "Sure! I guess all we need to do is ask them nicely, please, sir, would you stop hunting teeners?"

Zhene looked away and Ormandeau frowned, but De' Taurid stood and slapped Colossus, the crack of her hand against his cheek like a sudden thunderclap in the room. His suit reacted by closing space-tight transparent membrane over his face, a membrane that did nothing to hide the developing red mark that covered half his cheek.

"You pathetic little spoiled brat. I did not come here to listen to jokes." De' Taurid took Tammy's hand and started toward the dropshaft. "Chief Ormandeau, thank you for your suggestion, but I can see that this overgrown kindergarten is going to be no use to me."

Fade shrugged at Colossus. "She got ye number, boyo." To De' Taurid, she said, "Lady, don' let Big Stuff get under ye skin. Mouth not connect to brain, ye see? Scouts'll do what we can to help. Don' leave teeners in trouble."

"Please give us a chance," Legion said, then glared at Colossus.

Colossus, rubbing his sore cheek, slowly said, "I'm... sorry."

De' Taurid motioned Tammy to sit back down, then took her own seat. "I apologize. I'm overwrought. This situation disturbs me more than I can tell you."

Ormandeau shook his head. "The C.S.A. would never let you operate in the clear, so you'll have to go in as an undercover squad. Fortunately, it won't be hard to disguise most of you." His gaze lingered on BioLogic 17 and Mimic.

Mimic's body shimmered and expanded, until he became a perfect twin of Chief Ormandeau. "Mimic doesn't think he will have any problem," he said. "He can take on another form, if this one isn't satisfactory."

"I should know better," the Chief muttered.

"I," BioLogic 17 said, "will stay behind and do what I can to infiltrate the C.S.A. communication nets. I am sure that they are not as secure as the government thinks."

Zhene leaned forward. "If you do this, it'll be as private citizens, not as agents of the Myriad Worlds and definitely *not* as employees of Artveldt Enterprises." She frowned. "We'll give you what equipment and what help we can, but you're going to be largely on your own."

De' Taurid shook her head. "Not quite. We do have a few agents on the other side of the Curtain. I'll tell you how to get in touch with them. And I'll send what messages I can, telling them to be on the lookout for you."

Fade shrugged. "When we start?"

❖

The PsiScouts took a chartered transport from New York to Virginia. De' Taurid accompanied them, along with Tammy and Zhene.

"I have made some improvements in your gear," BioLogic 17 told them during the flight.

"Wish you could've made it more fashionable." Colossus looked ruefully down at his attire, conservative garments in the style of a previous century. "I feel like I'm going to a fancy-dress party."

Fade, looking ill-at-ease in a black, shin-length skirt and white sweater, wrinkled her nose. "How ye know about fashion, big boy? Take a class or something?" She held up one foot, showing a severe black boot with a four-centimeter heel. "Not looking forward to walkin' in these."

BioLogic 17 cleared his throat. "If I may have your attention...thank you. Your clothes were designed to fit in with the styles current in the C.S.A., but they are of the same impact-resistant fabric as your...playsuits." By the smug way he sat, BioLogic made it painfully obvious that he was the only one in normal clothes. "Your wristwatches conceal self-contained computers that are the equivalent of those you're used to. Unfortunately, you'll be out of touch with EarthNet —"

"What?!" Colossus shook his head. "No Net? Where are we supposed to get our information? How are we supposed to stay in touch?"

"—However," BioLogic continued, as if there had been no interruption, "You will find that most standard references are replicated in the units. For the data dump, we concentrated especially on information regarding the territories in which you'll be operating." He steepled his fingers and stared at the Scouts across them. "As for communication...you will be able to talk with one another as long as you're within a five-kilometer radius. Your standard earplants should work just fine." Legion unconsciously rubbed his right ear, where the tiny transceiver huddled invisibly in his ear canal. "You may be able to jack into ChristNet and whatever other networks you encounter, so long as they adhere to ISO-24.967.5 protocol."

"And how will we know if a network does?"

BioLogic considered the question for a moment, then shrugged. "Attempt to plug in. If you are successful, then you will know."

"An' if not," Fade said under her breath, "fried circuits."

De' Taurid handed each of them a flat plastic card covered with intricate designs. "These are C.S.A. crediplates; our hackers have fixed them so that they'll always show a balance of a few hundred dollars. That should be enough to take care of food, lodging, and transport."

Zhene looked each Scout full in the face, one after another. "I can't stress too strongly that the culture you're going into is traditional, rigid, and very distrustful of outsiders. Do you remember your aliases?"

"Jerry Allen," Colossus said, "Just spelled the old-fashioned way."

"Antonia Whitesell," Fade answered, wrinkling her nose.

"Lawrence Bragg," Legion said. With a twinkle in his eye, he added, "But everyone calls me Larry."

"Mimic is Reverend Kenneth Koroli."

"Good. Stick with your cover story and you should be okay. If they find out that you're from the outside, there's no telling what they might do to you."

"The Hunt," Tammy whispered. Legion shivered.

"Y-you know," Colossus said, "Maybe we should wait for Bolt and the others to get back."

Fade frowned. "Ye don' think we can do th' job, Big Boy?"

"No. It's just...th-they've had more experience at this kind of thing."

Fade's eyes raked the others. "Anyone else think like Big Boy? Want t' wait for founders?"

De' Taurid opened her mouth, but Zhene put a hand on her shoulder and she closed it.

"I don't know," Legion said. "This is pretty serious. We could get killed."

"If we choose to wait," Mimic said, "many others will perish."

"Tell ye what I think," Fade said with quiet intensity. "PsiScouts ain't Bolt or Coulomb or Mentaxa. PsiScouts is all of us. We every bit as good as them. Better, maybe." She touched Colossus's hand. "I make fun o'ye, Big Boy, but when ye keep defective brain out of th' way, ye do pretty good. Make us proud."

"Mimic agrees." The alien added his own stumpy, grey hand to Fade's and Colossus's. "Mimic has full faith in our team."

Legion reached out and joined his hand to the pile. "Okay. The PsiScouts Undercover Squad is on the job."

"Loj?"

BioLogic 17, with the air of pretending he was elsewhere, rested his hand atop the others. "Oh, all right. If team spirit will help you through this assignment, I add my encouragement."

The five teeners held their position for a moment, then Tammy shyly reached out and put her hand into the pile. "I-If it's okay, I'd like to come along with you."

De' Taurid pulled her back. "No!"

Tammy faced the older woman. "My friends are in danger, De' Taurid. Maybe some of them are dead already. If the PsiScouts are ready to risk everything to save them, I can't stay behind and do nothing."

"You won't be doing nothing. You'll be working with BioLogic to get them all the information they'll need."

"I can do that better if I'm there with them."

"Tammy, I am not going to let you back into the C.S.A. So you can just forget it."

Fade leaned toward De' Taurid. "All due respect, lady, but are ye Tammy's parent or somethin'?"

De' Taurid's eyes flared. "No. Her own parents didn't care enough about her to—"

"If ye ain't her parent, then ye got no right t' tell her what to do."

For the space of several heartbeats the two sat with eyes locked, De' Taurid and Fade, until De' Taurid released Tammy and looked away. "Fine. Do what you want." She glared at Fade. "But if you come back without her, I'll hold you fully responsible."

Fade put an arm around Tammy's shoulder. "If 'dults won't be responsible, guess teeners got to. So be it."

The transport banked and started descending. Zhene glanced at the viewscreen, where banks of blizzard-white cloud were racing up to envelop them. "Mimic?"

"Mimic is ready." The nonhuman's form blurred, shifted, and then was replaced by that of a heavyset Human man in his mid-forties: balding, dark-skinned, and clad in a severe black business suit. Around his neck was a collar of white as pure as the clouds. "Beg pardon. Reverend Koroli is ready."

Landing was uneventful, and at the jetport they bought C.S.A.-style clothes for Tammy to change into. De' Taurid had arranged a car, and they all piled in. Legion, squeezed between Mimic and Zhene in the back seat, kept his eyes on the scenery.

"What is this region called?" Mimic asked, in a deep baritone that fit Reverend Koroli's large frame.

"Shenandoah Valley," Zhene answered.

Tammy, nose pressed against the viewscreen, whispered, "It's beautiful."

It was indeed. Green, rolling farmland, crisscrossed by lazy-flowing streams, rose toward the east in a series of rounded hills. The horizon was dominated by great, sweeping mountains of dappled blue-green, ending in an uneven line where the pale blue sky met the deeper misty blue of distant treetops.

A narrow old road of overgrown macadam snaked up the mountainside; the driver followed it without even a glance of confirmation at De' Taurid. Soon, the sun was gone, and they moved silently through a green tunnel of living trees, bushes, ferns, and moss. The car, settling to only a half-meter above the surface, negotiated hairpin turns and broken slabs of asphalt steadily, but forward progress slowed until Legion almost believed he could walk faster. They passed a grazing deer, and all crowded to the viewscreen to take a look.

Suddenly they broke into sunlight at the crest of the mountain, and the driver steered the car into a broad gravel parking lot. "Here we are," he announced, allowing the car to settle to the ground. "Everybody out."

The PsiScouts needed no urging. They burst from the car and raced to the waist-high stone wall that surrounded the parking lot. Legion skidded to a stop, his stomach abruptly queasy—for beyond that stone wall was a sheer half-kilometer drop to the valley below.

Green and blue, lost in the misty distance, the Shenandoah Valley was spread out before them like an endless carpet. Legion caught his breath and shivered in the chill breeze.

"Look." Colossus pointed toward the crest. There, against the intense blue of the sky, was a group of three simple crosses, the center one slightly higher than the others. The tall one was pale blue, its companions yellow and green. Far to the right was another tiny trio, and when Legion looked left he was able to pick out a third trio on the top of the next mountain over.

Between the crosses, the air shimmered as if in summer heat. Legion tilted his head back, following the shimmer up into the sky. It seemed to extend without limit.

"What is it?" he whispered.

"The Curtain of Faith," Tammy answered. Legion could hear the capital letters.

BioLogic 17 beat the rest of them to the databank entry. "A force field erected by the Christian States in 2193 to separate their territory from the rest of the planet. The Curtain of Faith keeps the inhabitants inside, and prevents them from learning anything about the world beyond. From inside, the barrier is impassable except at well-defined border checkpoints. The effect continues three to four kilometers upward."

"Saint Bernard of Coffindaffer established the Curtain," Tammy said, "to keep us free from the temptations of the outside world. His sacred crosses mark the boundaries, and serve as a beacon for unbelievers to find their way to us."

There was an embarrassed silence, which Colossus finally broke. "Uh...okay, sure. Whatever. Are we going to stand here, or are we going closer?"

They climbed the hill, and Zhene pointed out a twisting stretch of broken asphalt and an ancient wooden sign that identified it as "The Blue Ridge Parkway." A rusty chain-link fence, three meters high and in places overgrown with vegetation, followed the course of the old road as it snaked along the mountaintops, at times only a few meters from the shimmer of the Curtain.

At intervals along the fence, glowing letters proclaimed: "WARNING. DO NOT CROSS FENCE. This area is beyond Myriad Worlds territory. Force field is one-way only. No return is possible at this location."

Legion shivered.

"What happens if someone strays over the line accidentally?" he asked.

"Usually they don't," De' Taurid answered. "Still, there's nearly ten thousand kilometers of border, and there's not a month that passes without us getting a frantic call from some parents whose kids went over on a dare, or some raft-riders or hikers stray over the line. Most of the time, the C.S.A. sends them back by way of Lynchburg or St. Louis or Dallas. They're not too interested in having any of our people who aren't already True Believers. Afraid of the ideas they might spread."

Fade glanced behind them, to the west. The sun was low, and lights were coming on in the valley. "Gettin' late. Better go." They planned to descend the mountains and move on to Lynchburg, some fifty kilometers away, under the cover of night.

De' Taurid lowered her eyes. "Remember the contact codes. We have friends in there. Good luck."

"Come back," Zhene said.

BioLogic nodded his confirmation. "I shall monitor the nets for your signals. When I break into ChristNet, I shall attempt to leave you a contact address."

Fade looked at the fence, then again at the sinking sun. "Right. Jetboards ready?"

She produced her own board, its compressed memplastic snapping into the rigid form it would maintain until touched in the right spot. Legion and Colossus loosed their own boards, set them to floating ten centimeters above the crumbling asphalt.

"Tammy, ye ride wi' me. Mimic, ye choice—can go wi' Legion or Big Boy."

"If it's all the same to you, Mimic will travel alone." His body shifted, taking on the form of a large, nondescript pigeon.

"Suit self. Big Boy, time to hop fence."

Colossus quickly grew until the fence was only waist-high. He picked up Tammy and Legion, stepped over the fence, and set them down.

While he was shrinking back to normal size, Fade walked through the fence and Mimic flew over it.

"Good luck," Zhene repeated.

The PsiScouts mounted their jetboards, and were gone.

❖

The road down the mountain was in much worse shape than the way up. What pavement remained was broken into twisted, crumbling slabs overgrown with weeds and heaved apart by strong saplings. Here and there, rows of yellow reflectors glinted in jet-board lights, marking hairpin turns and unsuspected drops. With Fade in the lead, the PsiScouts dodged trees and followed the meandering trail downward.

At first they chatted on the comm circuits, but soon the gathering darkness and the treacherous path occupied everyone's full concentration and chatter ended. There was nothing but the eerie, indistinct landscape rushing past, the swaying sensation of keeping a racing jetboard in balance. Beyond the lights and the broken roadway, was nothing—a void that could have been mountain, river, farmland, or sheer drop; there was no way to know.

Eventually, trees thinned out and a star-filled sky blossomed overhead. The road leveled out, becoming smoother at the same time. Legion relaxed, only then realizing how tense his muscles had been.

Behind, Legion sensed rather than saw the mountains, a hulking black-on-black shadow that blotted out the stars. The only illumination came from pale lights clustered in triples along the sky: the blue, yellow, and green of Saint Coffindaffer's crosses, defining the boundary through which there was now no return.

Fade's voice whispered in his ear, "Comm check. Legion, ye with us?"

"Still here." He stretched, sending his board skittering until he could recover. With a nervous chuckle, he asked, "How much longer to town?"

"Five more minutes," Colossus chanted.

"No, really."

"Maybe half hour," Fade said. "Tired?"

"I'll make it."

In a flapping of wings, a small bird descended to Fade's shoulder. Tammy looked alarmed and flinched as the bird perched there. "Mimic is getting tired. He never knew flying was so much work."

"You should have become a condor, buddy," Colossus laughed. "All they do is glide."

"Condor is too conspicuous, no?"

Legion agreed. "Condor is too conspicuous, yes." He maneuvered alongside Fade's board. "Tammy, how ya doing?"

Close up, Legion saw that the girl's face was white and her hands were knotted, arms around Fade's waist. "F-fine," she answered. "We're going pretty fast, aren't we?"

Legion didn't mention his feeling that they were only crawling along. "I guess you're not used to jetboarding?"

"Hey," Colossus called, swerving in front of them. "Don't hog the pretty girls all to yourself, Legion." He turned backwards on his board and flashed a toothy smile at Tammy. "If he's bothering you, just let me know."

"Lose testosterone, boys," Fade said with a flip of her head. "Lights ahead. Why?"

"Mimic will find out." With a sigh, the pigeon took to the air, and flew off toward a glow ahead of them.

"Rest break," Fade signaled, pulling off the road. Legion and Colossus followed.

The glow turned into actual lights, as if a vehicle were approaching from over the next hill. Presently Mimic returned, morphing into his guise of Reverend Koroli. "Mimic sees a car coming toward us. He suggests that we be ready for our first encounter."

"Can't we just hide until it passes?" Legion asked.

Fade shook her head. "Got to meet natives sooner or later. Better now, in dark and not crowded."

"I hope you're right."

"Faith, Legion-lad. Boards up, kids!"

With a practiced flip, Legion closed his jetboard. As the field which sustained it collapsed, carbon fiber curled into its neutral form; Legion had to help it with a little nudge, then the process was done and he was left with a thin disc about five centimeters across. Carefully avoiding the trigger-spot, he tucked it into his pocket.

The vehicle that descended upon them was a behemoth out of history vids, a wheeled monstrosity that lurched and growled, shivering every few seconds as if seized by convulsions. By the look of the huge tanks that made up most of its bulk, it burned some kind of fuel—alcohol?—instead of being connected to the power grids.

The vehicle staggered to a halt, pinning the PsiScouts in the baleful glare of its front-mounted floodlights. Seconds later, the noise ceased, and a tall man climbed down from the cab. He looked them up and down for a moment, then scratched his head. "What in creation are you kids doing here at this time of night?"

Mimic stepped forward, clearing his throat. "My son, perhaps you could tell me where we are?"

The man looked down. "I'm sorry, Reverend, I didn't see you there. I'm Caleb Johnson, and this is my farm. We're about twenty miles outside of Lynchburg, as the crow flies."

Mimic nodded, stroking his chin. Legion had to hold back laughter. "I see," Mimic said. "We were on a camping retreat in the mountains and lost our way. We seem to be quite a bit north of where I thought."

"Well praise the Lord I found you, Reverend! You go too much further north and you'll hit the Curtain, smack up against heathen lands."

"Yes. Praise the Lord indeed."

"Where are you and the youngsters headed?"

Mimic paused, then answered, "Denver, ultimately. Tonight we're on our way to Lynchburg."

The farmer held Mimic's eyes for the space of several heartbeats, and Legion didn't dare breathe. Then the man looked away. "Well, sir, I'm headed into town myself tonight for some shopping." He looked over the Scouts. "If you boys don't mind riding in the cargo compartment, I can give you a lift."

With a quick glance at Fade, Mimic smiled. "That would be wonderful, Mr. Johnson."

They shook hands. "Why don't you come inside, and we'll see what the Missus has on the stove for young appetites. After dinner, we'll head into town."

❖

Dinner was plentiful but plain, and "the Missus" did an excellent job of setting the visitors at their ease. The crowning touch was a fresh-baked apple pie, which Johnson assured them was made with apples from his own orchard. Colossus had two slices, and Legion allowed Mrs. Johnson to talk him into a third. When Mr. Johnson commented on his appetite, Mimic answered, "Sometimes we wonder if Larry is actually twins, the way he eats."

Legion managed to avoid choking on his pie.

After dinner, the teeners (at Mrs. Johnson's urging) took turns in the two bathrooms. As he was washing his hands, Legion heard Fade's voice from his communit. "Boyo?"

"Legion here."

"Fade. Listen. Ye trust Farmer Johnson?"

"Sure. Why not?"

"Don' know. Not sure." He could almost see her frown. "Boyo, ye mind doin' something for me?"

"What?"

"Split up. One of ye hang back, out of sight, follow truck to town on jetboard? In case trouble?"

"Aw, Fade, I'm tired—"

"Please?"

He stopped. It was the first time he'd heard Fade say that word. All at once, he realized how she must feel: lonely, scared, bearing the awful burden of uncertainty in running this mission—and just as suddenly, he felt ashamed of his own selfishness. "Okay. You're right, we don't know for sure and we're not safe until we're back home. I'll split."

"Thank ye, boyo."

Under his breath, Legion muttered, "But I don't have to like it." Then he split in two, sent his double back to the dining room, and carefully let himself out of the house without being seen. He crouched in bushes near the truck, waiting.

❖

Legion number two climbed into the truck's cargo compartment and sat on the corrugated metal floor next to Colossus. There wasn't enough room to stand or to stretch out, but the two boys would be perfectly comfortable sitting.

"It won't be long," Johnson said, then slammed the hatch and waved through its narrow window.

As soon as he moved away, Legion tried the hatch. "Locked," he said.

Colossus shrugged. "So we won't fall out. Good." He scrunched into a corner and closed his eyes. "I'm going to try to take a nap."

"Go ahead."

Legion's communit came to life. "Fade here. Gonna leave this channel open so ye can hear what goes on." The truck rocked, doors slammed, and then the engine roared to life. After a few moments, the truck lurched forward.

❖

Legion number one watched the others board the truck and heard Fade's announcement. Then, as the truck began moving, he sprang forward, snapping his jetboard out at the same time. Avoiding the rear-view mirrors, he grabbed the back of the truck and pulled himself up. A short ladder led him to a cargo rack on the roof; he pulled a dirty canvas cover over himself, then thumbed his communit to minimum volume. He hoped Fade knew what she was doing.

❖

The land descended further, and scattered lights of houses grew more numerous. Colossus was softly snoring; Legion soon stopped looking out the window and put his head back, listening to the farmer's endless and pointless anecdotes. His other self, safe atop the truck, had checked in via communit; all was well. Legion closed his eyes, letting the rollicking motion of the truck lull him into a contented daze.

He jerked awake and crawled to the window. They had reached the city; bright advertising signs split the night with garish primary colors, spelling out their messages for all viewers: "Christ is Lord," "Repent Now—Reasonable Rates," and "Church of Life Eternal: Over Fifty Million Saved." The symbol of the cross was everywhere.

Legion shook Colossus's shoulder. "We're almost there."

The road was crowded with other vehicles of all shapes and sizes. The truck seemed to crawl along, stopping every few moments, then gliding forward for a time. Farmer Johnson sounded like a tour guide: "That's the biggest church in Lynchburg...they baptize over a thousand people each week. There's the house where Saint Falwell lived. See how clean the streets are? Every congregation takes care of a few blocks; you can see their signs if you look. There's one. The womenfolk plant these gardens; there's quite a bit of competition for the prettiest."

"It's a lovely city," Mimic said in his Reverend Koroli voice.

"Have you paid your respects to Saint Falwell yet?"

"Pardon?"

"Saint Falwell's monument...right over there." The truck slowed and made a sweeping right turn. "The Saint's body remains there to this day, just as it was when he died. Every visitor to Lynchburg must see him. It's good luck. It will take you only a moment, but you'll remember it for the rest of your life. No, I insist." The truck stopped in a parking lot; a few meters away, steep stone steps led to a small Greek temple atop a hill.

"Tell me just one thing, Reverend Koroli?"

"Yes?"

"Why did you think I'd believe that a man of the cloth would take boys and girls on a camping trip together? Without any further adult supervision?"

"Er...You're saying that you don't believe Reverend Koroli?"

"I don't know who you are or what you're up to, but you have sixty seconds to get out of my truck and turn yourself over to those policemen in front of the monument."

❖

Fade knew in the pit of her stomach that things were going wrong.

Mimic sputtered, Tammy shivered, and Fade drew back against the door of the truck. Wrong, wrong, this wasn't how things were supposed to happen. Taurid's fault, for not giving them enough background. Mimic's fault, for not doing a better job of impersonating a Reverend. Tammy's fault, for getting them involved in this smelly business in the first place.

Fade's fault, for not being a better leader.

She stabbed her communit and shouted, "Bail out!" Then, throwing all her weight against the door, she tugged at the handle. The door flew open, and Fade tumbled to the ground, pulling Tammy after her.

"Reverend Koroli wishes he could stay around and talk," Mimic said. Then he morphed into a large bird and shot past Fade, wings beating. He gained altitude and was rapidly lost in the night.

Fade pushed Tammy to her feet. "Go, girl! Get out of here!"

From nowhere, Legion dropped in front of her. "I'll take her. You get Colossus and me free." He split into five, and each one hopped on his own jetboard. One of them grabbed Tammy, and then they were off in different directions.

Farmer Johnson lunged across the seat, and Fade let herself go intangible. The man scrambled down from the truck, his hands passing through her as if she were composed of mist.

The truck walls were no obstacle to her. Colossus and Legion were crouched at the back of the cargo compartment, peering out the single tiny window; she cleared her throat and they turned.

"We heard," Legion said. "What do we do now?"

"Split up. Run. Regroup later."

"That's easy for you to say." Colossus pushed against the cargo hatch. "We're locked in."

Fade stuck her head out of the truck for a moment. Johnson was running toward the monument, and half a dozen uniformed guards were headed in his direction. She popped her head back in. "Police on the way. Grow, big boy!"

Colossus spread his hands. "I can't. The metal's too strong. I'll just end up crushing both of us."

"Then what good are ye? Legion, can't merge with one of other selves?"

"Through a steel wall? No."

"Can't break lock, can't smash walls, ye can't walk through matter…boys, can't get ye out."

"What are you going to do?" Colossus said. "You can't leave us here."

"Gonna have to. Johnson will open truck. After that, run when ye can. We follow you." She let herself fade into invisibility. "Ye got friends, we ain't gonna give ye up. We'll help."

With that, the hatch opened. Six guards stood outside, with weapons poised. Farmer Johnson rubbed his hands. "At least you two won't be running away."

One of the guards gestured with his gun. "Come on down, boys. You're coming with us."

❖

Legion-one, with Tammy hugging his waist, steered his jetboard between buildings and down a narrow alley, then skidded to a stop behind a tree in a large concrete pot. No one from the street could see them here.

"Now we're really in trouble," Tammy said. "Th-those were Army of God troops. You're supposed to obey them instantly."

"Yeah, well, I'm going through a disobedient phase right now." He touched his communit, scowled at its display. "Too many signals." He punched another code, and the holographic display unfolded from his wrist like a flower opening to the sun. At ten centimeters across, it was much easier to read.

Four scattered signals from his own dopplegangers, another that bore Fade's ID code...and two close together, Colossus and Legion-two, still at the site of the monument. They had not escaped.

"They've got two of us," he said. "Where do these Army of God people take their prisoners?"

"How should I know? I've never been to Lynchburg in my life."

Legion took a breath. "Sorry, I didn't mean it that way."

"That's okay, you're worried about your friends." She frowned. "Let me think. Army of God are national troops, not local police. They probably have a base somewhere outside the city."

"That doesn't exactly help."

"I know. Don't you have maps of the city?"

Legion glanced at his wristwatch. "Yeah. But I don't have any idea what I'm looking for." He thumbed the communit. "Fade? What's up?"

He heard the rush of air as she answered. "Little busy, boyo. Tailin' cop car on m' jetboard."

There was a click, and Mimic joined the conversation. "Mimic thinks we don't have to worry as long as Colossus and Legion are wearing their communits. BioLogic said we could track them up to five kilometers."

"Jus' hope they ain't going further." Legion almost heard her shrug. "All right, I'm pullin' over. Now, anybody got any ideas what to do? Tammy, what ye say?"

"Why does everybody keep asking me? I don't know!"

"Grip, girl. Jus' asking. Legion? How many of ye on the loose?"

"Five. Plus the one with Colossus."

"We should have 'em confused, then. That's somethin'. Damn, wish we knew more. Where Colossus and Legion going, how well guarded, what's gonna happen to 'em?"

"Perhaps," Mimic said, "this would be a good time to call on one of De' Taurid's contacts."

"Am not exactly in mood to trust another 'dult," Fade growled.

"We are not exactly in a position to refuse any aid."

"He's right," one of the Legions said.

There was a long pause, then Fade said, "Right. Still don' like it. Ever'body safe, hidden, all that?"

The others all reported that they were safely hidden. Legion glanced at the street, where a steady stream of vehicles passed in sublime indifference, and agreed.

"Good," Fade said. "Lookin' at contact list. Only one in Lynchtown. Netcode, nothing else."

"Well?"

"Legion—ye call. Ye talk their talk better'n us."

As one, five Legions sighed. One of them said, "Who's one?"

Legion, ignoring Tammy's bewildered look, answered, "I am, I guess."

"How ye know?"

"We decide when I split." Legion was tired of explaining to people how he kept order among himself. "Watch sometime, and you'll see each of me hold up fingers from one to six. We keep those numbers until we come together again."

"Elegant," Mimic said.

"Whatever. Now will everybody please be quiet? I have a call to make."

❖

The netcode that de' Taurid had given them was answered by an artificially-disguised voice and no video. The person— or possibly it was a 'bot—cautioned them not to discuss anything sensitive on the net. "Come to the Public Library," it directed. "Tell them at the main desk that you have come to pick up materials for Mr. North. That is all."

"Okay-okay," Fade said. "Map says Memorial Avenue, outside town. Ten-fifteen minutes max. Get together before we enter. Go!"

Legion jumped on his jetboard and helped Tammy climb aboard behind him. "On our way," he cried; then the jets caught and they were gone.

❖

The Public Library was a run-down, one-story building in the middle of an overgrown, parklike expanse. When Legion arrived he found Fade waiting, concealed behind a thicket. As his other selves showed up, one by one, he merged with them. Mimic, as a large sparrow, was the last to arrive. As soon as he landed, he morphed into the form, not of Reverend Koroli, but of a rather ordinary-looking dark-haired teener boy dressed in the same conservative clothes as the others. He grimaced, and Legion frowned in sympathy. These changes were uncomfortable for Mimic, he knew—and too many in a short space of time could be downright painful.

A pleasant, somewhat musty odor greeted them as they entered through frosted-glass doors. Legion sneezed.

In the dim light the building seemed to be one large expanse, divided into numberless small alcoves by a haphazard arrangement of shelves upon shelves. Toward the center were a few tables, where anonymous 'dults worked in pools of light. Together, the PsiScouts advanced toward a high counter at the far end of the room, where a faded sign read: "Information Desk."

Shelves everywhere—and as Legion's eyes adjusted to the gloom, he was able to discern what sat upon all those shelves. In rows and piles and heaps, all obviously organized according to some scheme he could not fathom, they were… books. The place was a museum of books.

The coin-sized casings of bookdots were everywhere, but Legion also saw disc-books, reels and cards of filmbooks, two dozen different styles of talking books, peculiar oblong packages that had to be early holobooks—he was not surprised to see case upon case of actual paper books, arranged in impeccable order and well-maintained.

A red-faced little gnome of a man, balding and clad in a bright emerald suit, looked up from the counter as they approached. His eyes questioned without his mouth having to do any work.

Fade elbowed Legion forward. He cleared his throat. "Ah…we're here to pick up…er…something for Mr. North."

The gnome looked to left and right; none of the patrons seemed to be paying any attention. "Quickly, come with me," he said, heading off through a door into the darkened spaces behind the counter.

Fade shrugged and led the PsiScouts after the man.

The back room had none of the ordered arrangement of the shelves out front. Unsteady stacks of books, reading equipment, and unidentifiable junk rose from every surface and buttressed every wall. One alcove was set up as a tiny kitchen with a table and a few chairs; a side door led to an antiquated lavatory. A single terminal that looked like something out of a historical holoshow was balanced on a narrow wooden desk in the center of the space. The librarian perched on a rickety stool before it.

"I'm Ed Hill," he announced. "I suppose you're the kids that the Police are looking for?"

"Wh-what makes you think that?"

He touched the screen and pages of text scrolled by. "I'm tapped into the Police nets, of course." He narrowed his eyes. "Where are the others?"

"Police got 'em," Fade answered.

Hill shook his head. "No, I mean the others who ran from Monument Hill. The police reported between six and eight teenagers. I see four."

"Four is all." Fade looked from Mimic to Legion. "Rest was…done with mirrors."

"I understand." Ed Hill leaned back in his chair, almost raising his feet off the floor. "What do you want?"

"Huh?"

"The only people who ever call on the code you used are people who need help. I take it you're from the outside, on business that we needn't discuss. What kind of help do you need?"

"Need to know where cops're taking our buddos. 'N how to get 'em back."

"Let me see." Hill turned to the terminal, expertly tapping his fingernail against the screen with a staccato of clicks. After a minute he turned and gave them a frown. "Your two friends are in detention at the Armory of God just across the river. They're being charged as deserters."

"Deserters? From what?"

"From the Christian Youth." At their blank faces, he continued, "Service is mandatory for everyone under eighteen. Your friends, obviously, are not on file with any Christian Youth chapter in the nation." He read more from the screen. "They're scheduled to go out on the first train in the morning, which will be…" more clicking, "…five-thirty."

"Going where?"

"To detention camp in Denver. Problem youth from everywhere are sent there for training."

Fade turned to Tammy. "Is that where…?"

Tammy, pale, only nodded.

"What?" Ed Hill's face grew redder. "What did I say?"

"Our friends are gonna be hunted down and killed."

"I hardly think that detention camp is *that* bad. It's received many good reviews in the press." He stopped suddenly. "Ah. I see." The flush of his cheeks grew deeper, and his mouth tautened into an angry line. "This is not the first time that our government has lied to us. I presume you have different information about the detention camp?"

Legion stepped forward, putting an arm around Tammy's shoulders. "We have a survivor."

"I see. This will certainly change our agender."

Fade raised her wrist. "Scouts, it's time we talk to our buddos."

❖

The jail cell was six paces by eight…at least in Colossus's stride. After two hours of watching his friend ceaselessly pacing, Legion knew the numbers well.

"You might as well sit down," Legion said at last, patting the hard plastic bench that occupied most of one cinderblock wall. "In fact, why don't you take a nap? You've *got* to be tired."

Colossus didn't sit down, but he did stop pacing and leaned against the wall. "There has to be a way out of here."

"There is." Legion hooked his thumb at the one steel door. "Sooner or later someone will unlock it."

Colossus crouched next to him. "You're right. When they do, I'll get as big as I can, and you split so that—"

Legion shook his head. "I'm already split. One of me is all you get this time."

"Okay, nada problem, I can still—"

"Gery, give it up, okay? We aren't going to break out of here on our own. Even if we get out of this cell, you think we could fight our way past all those police officers? Stunners and tanglers are bad enough, but some of them were packing real lasers."

Colossus picked up a palm-sized display pad, and idly clicked past luridly-illustrated religious tracts. "Then what are we going to do?"

"Wait." He idly touched his right ear. The police had taken their clothing and wristwatch-computers, dressed the boys in drab grey, too-large coveralls—but they had missed the implanted communits. Maybe they hadn't even known to look.

"Oh, I get it—"

"Good," Legion hastily interrupted Colossus, directing his eyes toward a camera perched in a corner. To his relief, Colossus gave a nod and shut up. Unfortunately, he went back to pacing.

It was only a few minutes later that Legion's communit clicked on. Fade said, "Legion? Colossus? Anybody home?"

Legion caught Colossus's eyes. He was sure that the cops were watching and listening, and would come in at once if they realized the boys were in communication with their friends. Yet they had to answer Fade.

Colossus grinned and his face lit up. He lowered himself to his knees, pulling Legion down on the hard floor next to him. "Yes, Lord," Colossus said, "we, your humble servants, await your word."

Keeping his head down to cover his own smile, Legion said, "Speak to us, O Lord."

He could see Fade shaking her head. "Ye crazy, or what?"

"Even though we are imprisoned by our enemies, Lord, they cannot keep us from hearing your word; nor can they keep our pleas from reaching your ears." Once he started, Legion found that it was easy enough to keep us this sort of patter.

"Give us your counsel, Master," Colossus intoned. "What shall we do?"

"I get it," Fade said. "Ye're scheduled on morning train to Denver. Want ye to go peaceful."

Legion wrinkled his brow. "Er...Lord, I do not understand."

"We tail ye, right? Got tickets for same train. Ye go to detention camp, scope out. On way, we contact De' Taurid's helpers in Denver, set up rescue or whatever."

Legion and Colossus exchanged glances, then Legion replied, "This is a difficult task you set for us, Lord. But we will try to be worthy of your trust."

Fade snorted. "Quit sweet-talk and go sleep. See ye in Denver."

❖

Ed Hill arranged for their tickets to Denver, then told the Scouts they should get some sleep. He produced some ancient sleeping bags and spread them out in opposing corners of the small back room. Legion noted wryly that he carefully put the girls as far as possible from the boys.

"I'll do my best to track down everything I can about the detention camps," he said, "and I'll have it on a disk for you in the morning. Meanwhile, you should try to rest. You won't have much chance to sleep on the train."

Legion crawled into the musty sleeping bag and curled into his favorite position, but sleep wouldn't come. Deep within, he felt the ache of his missing self, an incompleteness that was midway between the sensations of hunger and physical pain. The room was dark, except for the dim glow of Ed Hall's terminal; silent, except for the tapping of keys and Mimic's steady breathing beside him. His mind drifted over the events of the day—the hypnotic jetboard ride down the mountain, Farmer Johnson's betrayal, the different parts of the city his five selves had seen when they fled. All the while, shadow sensations danced just below the threshold of thought, and he fancied that he was somehow perceiving and echo of what the jailed Legion witnessed...even though he knew that was impossible.

He remained still and quiet, letting all the memories and sensations wash over him, until eventually the darkened room blurred into the Johnson's kitchen... except that instead of Farmer Johnson and his wife, Legion's own parents sat at the massive wooden table, and his father was shaking his head while Mother told him how disappointed in him they were. "We should never have sent a boy to do a man's job," she said. Behind him, out of sight no matter how he turned, there was the sound of running water...a trickle that became a torrent that became a rushing flood. Through his mother's scolding and his father's disappointed tears, Legion understood that he was supposed to stop the water—but instead, he had only lost his tools, lost his clothes (he noticed that he was naked), lost his whole house. And what was worse, he'd also lost...well, he didn't know what else he'd lost, but he knew it was the worst thing of all.

And all this time the water continued flowing, bursting forth from a dozen new leaks every minute, swirling across the kitchen floor and around his ankles—except it wasn't water, it was a fluid darker and more viscous, which clung to his calves and left marks where it splashed on his belly and arms, warm against his bare skin, and as the level continued to rise he finally recognized it as...blood.

Then his mother and father were gone, replaced by the hollow-eyed corpses of anonymous teeners, and as Legion sat rooted to his chair, unable to turn around or close his eyes, he heard behind him the rustle and splash of an approaching creature...a creature, Legion knew, from whose bony claws dangled the lifeless body of the thing he had lost. As the warm, swirling blood rose over his knees, he felt hot breath on the back of his neck, and then the creature's hand, rough and dry like sandpaper, on his unprotected shoulder—

Legion bolted awake and saw Ed Hill leaning over him, the old man's hand on his shoulder. "Wake up, boy. You have to hide. The police are coming here."

"Wha—?"

Fade, hands on hips, and two sleeping bags over her shoulders, looked down at him. "Cops, buddo. Time to crawl down a hole."

Legion pulled himself out of the sleeping bag, licked dry lips, and struggled to his feet. Mimic, still in the guise of a dark-haired teener boy, was already awake and held a trembling Tammy.

Ed Hill gestured. "Follow me. Bring the sleeping bags."

He shoved aside a pile of dusty boxes and lifted a battered trapdoor that they had concealed. Beneath was a narrow, dark space festooned with cobwebs and hardly deep enough to stand up in; a precarious stepladder seemed the only way down.

"In you go," he said. "And stay there until I come to get you. It won't be comfortable for the four of you, but at least the cops won't find you."

Fade threw the two sleeping bags she carried down, then became half-transparent. "Legion, take Tammy. Mimic, can ye do something small? Mouse or bug or whatnot?"

Mimic took a deep breath, screwed up his face in pain, and folded in upon himself until he was a small, scraggly tomcat with mousey fur and a notched left ear. Some stray he had met during his stay on Earth, Legion decided. Mimic, managing to look thoroughly delighted with himself, licked a paw and then sprang up to the top of a stack of boxes.

Ed Hill raised an eyebrow, but said nothing. Fade, growing more indistinct with each passing second, pointed down the hole. "Go."

Tammy peered down dubiously. "You first."

"All right." Legion lowered himself to the rickety stool, then hopped down to concrete floor. He held up his arms and guided Tammy down.

"I'll get rid of them as soon as I can," Ed Hill said. "There should be a torch hanging on the wall." With that, he lowered the trapdoor and Legion heard the sound of boxes sliding back into place.

He felt along a bare cinderblock wall until he found a cylinder hanging from a nail; when he touched a switch on its side, the cylinder blossomed with cold, white light, about as bright as a full moon. It filled the chamber, except where their inky shadows fell. Legion moved the torch slowly, panning around the cramped space.

Bookshelves lined the walls, bookshelves crammed with spools and disks and bookdots, fiche cardsets and leatherbound paper books. He silently scanned the titles: Plato's *Republic*. The complete works of Shakespeare, Tiptree, Kipling, Twain, King. *The Federalist Papers. Stranger in a Strange Land. Great Expectations. Gulliver's Travels. A Brief History of Time. The Encyclopedia Britannica. The Left Hand of Darkness. Structured Programming. Common Sense. The Rig-Veda. The Lord of the Rings. Brewer's Dictionary of Phrase and Fable. Trouble and Her Friends. The Golden Bough. Principia Mathematica. The Bhagavad-Gita. The Constitution of the Martian Confederation.* Classics, all of them...and from the faded, cracked packages, all of them centuries old.

Tammy whistled quietly. "These books are all forbidden."

"Forbidden?"

"It's against the law to read them, or even to have them in your possession." She hesitantly ran her fingers along the binding of the Shakespeare volume. "I saw this one once in Denver. Some of the kids found a copy on disk. We used to act out parts at night, when no one was around to hear us."

"You're kidding. I studied most of these in basic school. They're all on the nets."

Tammy sat down on the concrete floor, pulled her knees up under her chin. "Now you see why I ran away from home and went to Denver."

Legion joined her on the floor; it was more comfortable than crouching. "It must have been terrible."

"You don't know. You can't. Where I grew up, in Arkansas, everybody expected you to do exactly what all the other kids did—which was what their parents did, and *their* parents, and so on back to the beginning of time. Bible school, cotillion, Christian Youth, then find a nice boy and settle down with him, raise a family, send your kids to Bible school and cotillion and football games and Christian Youth." She closed her eyes. "Nobody said or did or thought anything that hadn't been said or done or thought a million times before, and if you *did* you were a freak, a disgrace to your friends and your family."

"So you ran away."

"Uh-huh. With my girlfriend, Paula. We had some money, so we bought tickets to Denver."

"Why there?"

She stared as if he'd said something stupid. "Denver... Denver's where everything happens. Where the government is. All the glamorous people live there. It's where they make all the virties. They always say, all roads lead to Denver. Who wouldn't want to go there?"

Legion nodded. "I've viddied some virties out of your country." He didn't have the heart to tell her that they were the most insipid, dull, and pointless virtual reality productions he'd witnessed...nor that a popular EarthNet comedian routinely put them up (with appropriate commentary) for laughs.

Almost inaudible footsteps sounded above, and Tammy looked up nervously. She whispered, "What'll we do if they find us?"

"They won't." He moved closer to her. "Finish telling me about Denver."

She looked past his shoulder, and he knew she was seeing the past. "It was great, at first. See, Denver is a whole bunch of different groups, and they don't have that much to do with one another. There's the rich people, and the virtie crowd, and the politicians...and then there's the kids." She smiled. "Troublemakers, rebels, freaks—my kind of people. There's whole areas of the city that are abandoned, and the kids have it all organized. Every group is in a different building. Like families."

Legion nodded. "Gangs." Wherever there were kids, anywhere in the Galaxy, they formed gangs. It was a law of nature.

"No, more than that. We took care of one another."

"So what happened?"

"The hunters."

Legion was suddenly uncomfortably aware of the scars that Tammy wore, the ordeal she had been through. "I-I'm sorry. If you don't want to talk about it—"

"No, it's okay. I don't really remember that much, to tell the truth. I was out of my head a lot of the time, I guess."

"How did you...get involved? I mean, how do they—?"

"The Hunt is a big thing...I almost said 'in Denver,' but it's big all through the country. Once a month, except in the winter. Hunters sign up years in advance. There are lotteries where you can win a place as a hunter. 'Course, they never say *what* they're hunting. Just that the herds need thinning, this time there are so many head to be terminated." She gave a forced chuckle. "I guess I always thought it was deer or buffalos or something. Not...kids."

Above, there was a thump, and then a sliding sound as if boxes were being moved aside. Tammy huddled against Legion, hiding her face against his chest. He shifted his weight and put his arms around her, trying to offer whatever comfort he could.

"They're coming," she whispered. "They know we're here."

"Shh." He clicked off the torch. "It's going to be all right." He gripped the torch firmly. It wasn't much of a weapon, but it was better than throwing books at them.

The trapdoor lifted, light blinded him...and then Ed Hill said, "You can come out now. The cops are gone. We've seen the last of them until morning—and by that time, you'll be halfway to Denver."

❖

It was a most uncomfortable train ride. Legion and Colossus were fitted with restraining anklets: they could wander their train car freely, but at any attempt to leave, the anklet would sound an alarm and deliver an incapacitating electrical shock. Colossus slipped into the lavatory to attempt to grow out of the anklet; he returned to report that it would sever his leg before it broke.

A police officer, ostensibly along to guard the boys, stretched out in his seat and went to sleep as soon as they pulled out of Lynchburg. With a grey dawn filling the sky, the train climbed swiftly up the mountains to the south, then leapt forward along a pair of gleaming tracks suspended above the verdant land on graceful trestles. Soon the scenery was a blur of indistinct green-grey, the only constant being the arrow-straight line of tracks ahead and behind.

Colossus nodded toward the guard in the seat behind them. "He's got the right idea." With a mighty stretch and a huge yawn, he settled back and closed his eyes.

Legion peered up and down the length of the car. "I hope the others got on."

His ear implant clicked on, and Fade said softly, "We here, boyo. Monitoring your sets."

Colossus grunted. "Yeah, well, keep it down. I'm trying to sleep."

"Got up on wrong side of bed, eh?" She chuckled. "Tell ye what, Big Boy, I cut ye out of circuit if ye promise not to leave Legion's side."

"Whatever." Colossus turned his back, ignoring them.

"I'm glad to hear from you," Legion whispered. "What's going on?"

"Cops were after us, but we slipped 'em. Still tryin' to figure how to spring you boys."

"The police," Mimic said, "do not seem to expect organization from kids. This is perhaps our greatest advantage."

"Were you planning on doing something before we get to Denver?"

"Don' see how we can, boyo. Got any ideas?"

Legion lowered his head. "No."

"We keep thinkin', ye do same. Meantime, listen up. Ye other self want Tammy-girl t' tell her story."

He sat back and closed his eyes, listening as Tammy related her tale of running away to Denver and finding a place in the teener underground there.

"The hunt is big," she said, "and this was the Easter Hunt...the biggest ever. We heard on the news that there were over ten thousand hunters in town for it. None of us kids wanted to believe that—one thousand is usual, and they try to make sure that each hunter can get at least one... trophy."

Legion's stomach, already uneasy due to the train's uneven sway, lurched. He clamped his jaw and kept his eyes firmly closed.

"Well, that Thursday they started rounding us up. Usually there's a kind of truce between the cops and the kids...once a month they would make a show of cruising through the abandoned areas, and any kid who was caught in the open would be shipped off to the Detention Camps. But you learned to watch out for that, not to be out when they came by."

"This time was different?" Legion heard himself ask.

"This time they came in force, and they meant business. They broke into the buildings, they tracked us down, they caught us with stunners and tanglewebs. We were crammed into trucks, packed like parcels, a hundred kids or more in each truck. As soon as one was full, it took off, and they started loading the next one. This went on all night.

"The trucks took us into the Pike Forest, where there was a sort of campsite. The kids who were there already unloaded us, cut us loose from the tanglewebs, took care of the ones who were stunned. After it got dark, trucks of food started coming, and then a bunch of us kept busy unloading them and making sure everybody got fed."

"Was there no adult supervision? No buildings? Sanitary facilities?" In his human guise, Mimic's normally-flat voice was intense and agitated.

"Nothing but a big ol' fence around the whole campsite, and police with real guns outside it." Bitterly, Tammy said, "We kids had been taking care of each other without adult supervision for a long time—we just kept it up, that's all. At first the gangs tried to stay together, but it was too crazy for that...so everybody pitched in wherever they could help. We got some fires started and shelters built, and after a while someone found crates of blankets mixed in with the food shipments.

"By Saturday night the trucks stopped coming. We held a meeting in a clearing, and some of the older kids told everyone what was going to happen. A lot of kids cried. In the end, we just had a big prayer meeting, when we all asked God to take care of us."

There was silence for a few moments, as if no one dared to ask the next question. Then Tammy continued her story without prompting. "Early Sunday morning the fence was torn down, and adults came to make us scatter. We...uh, we knew that if we stayed at the camp, we wouldn't stand a chance at all."

"A chance of what?" Legion whispered.

"The forest is right up against the Curtain of Faith. At Red Hill Pass, about twenty miles away, there's an old tunnel that goes through the mountain and under the Curtain. Ordinarily the tunnel is closed, but not during the Hunt. The way the Hunt is arranged, any kids who can get to that tunnel is allowed through...into the outside world, safe and sound. All of us kids knew that. And all of us, one way or another, would be making for that tunnel."

"Mimic wonders how long the Hunt lasted. And what happened to teeners who survived until the end?"

"The Hunt went on until every hunter bagged a trophy. Usually it was over by the next morning." Tammy paused. "I-I don't know what happened if you managed to survive. I never met anyone who did. The whole area was cordoned off with a low-power Curtain. But I guess someone could hide in the woods until they let the field down. Like I say, I never heard of anybody who survived."

"Might not head back to city. What next?"

"The Hunt started right on schedule. The hunters were armed with projectile guns and lasers, whatever they could carry. In the first hour, I saw more than a hundred kids shot down, zap, just like that." She took a breath. "I ran into this girl I knew, Jeanne. She was leading a dozen or so kids; they were headed for the tunnel. Jeanne seemed to know what she was doing. She had us head south, over the hills, then cut west in a section of the forest that was really dense. I think she was following some kind of trail, but if it was marked I couldn't see how."

"She from city?" Fade asked.

"I think so. At least, I'd seen her there every once in a while. We kept going; we ran into one hunter, and he winged a boy named Jules. So we took turns carrying Jules. By the time it was getting dark, we were on the hillside above Red Hill Pass. The tunnel looked unguarded, but Jeanne said we should wait until late at night. Then one or two of us would slip through at a time."

"What went wrong?"

"A bunch of hunters were waiting in the trees...maybe ten or twelve of them, scattered all around. One of them must've noticed us, because the next minute they were all firing on us." Tammy sighed. "I know I was hit. I remember Jeanne picked me up and was running with me. I was so tired, and I hurt so much. Then I don't remember much else, until I found myself on the mountains, in snow, and your medics found me."

"That was outside the Curtain, right?"

"Yes. I must've made it through, I don't know how. I don't know how many others did."

"Mimic suspects it was few, if any. Infrared scans would certainly have noticed them the same way Tammy was noticed."

"Thing t' do," Fade mused, "is chat with Jeanne. If can find her."

"If she wasn't...a victim," Tammy said.

There seemed no answer to that.

❖

Roanoke, Johnson City, Knoxville, Nashville...the cities, long forgotten in the outside world, raced past. Across the aisle, four preteener girls sang, badly and loudly, while their ineffectual 'dult guardians chatted on, mindless and oblivious. To pass the time, Legion fumbled with the vidscreen in the back of the seat before him.

It was plain receive-only flat video, no Net access and no virtie plugs, only three channels and none of them news or reference. There wasn't even a keyboard, real or virtual. Legion almost gave up on the thing in disgust, but then the girls started their twenty-third round of "Jesus Loves Me" and he turned to the screen in relief.

The programs, by and large, were little twenty-minute melodramas, most of them obviously designed to teach some sort of moral lesson. Visions, miracles, and angelic visitors were frequent; one ongoing series concerned the adventures of a pair of misfit angels who travelled around the country doing good deeds.

The commercials were almost as interesting as the shows they interrupted. Without exception, the products advertised were certified by a bishop and blessed by God (who seemed to have an excessive interest in preventing or covering up body odors.)

The most chilling commercial was one that reminded hunters that there were still a few spaces open for the National Hunt in Colorado this weekend. In a tasteful montage of woodland images, the commercial touted fresh air and the thrill of the hunt, without ever mentioning the nature of the prey. Any registered hunter, it said, could reserve a space for only a thousand dollars (Legion didn't know if that represented a great sum of money, although from the other prices he'd heard, it would buy an awful lot of toothpaste and underarm deodorant.)

"Guys," he whispered.

"Here," Fade answered.

"Were you just watching the vid? There's going to be a Hunt this weekend."

There was a pause, then Fade said, "Da, ye right. Starts Sunday morning."

"And today's Wednesday."

"Da."

A cold place opened up in the pit of his stomach. "So if Colossus and I don't get out of that detention camp in the next four days...we're dead."

"We be working on some ideas, Buddy Boy. Grip yeself. Ye not gonna die."

"That's easy for you to say. What ideas?"

Legion's other self calmly answered, "You've been watching their video. You *must* see the possibilities."

That stopped him. The cold place in his stomach started to warm up.

Slowly, Legion began to smile.

❖

Memphis...Little Rock...Fort Smith. They hardly seemed to pause at each station. Oklahoma City...Dodge City...Lamar...and, finally, the train hissed to a halt in a station marked simply: Denver. Carried by the crowd like leaves by an onrushing stream, the kids moved up broad stairs—all but Fade, who stayed behind to make sure Legion and Colossus were okay. After a few minutes she reported by comm, "They all right. Guard follow them out, into cop car, take off. That's it." She reappeared, stepping from behind a massive granite column. "Off we go."

Mimic took on his Reverend Koroli form and waved at a taxi. It landed and the kids piled in. Legion was shocked to see that the cab was not automatic; a slim, dark-haired man sat at the controls, separated from the passenger compartment by a thick transparent shield.

"Praise the Lord. Where to?" the man asked.

Mimic didn't hesitate. "Praise the Lord. We need a reasonable hotel near the center of town. Someplace decent, where the children will be safe."

"Got it. You want the Damascus House, then, Reverend." The cab lifted off.

The Damascus House was a towering edifice of orange-yellow plascrete, steel, and glass; in the setting sun it glowed like a pillar of fire. Mimic—knowing by now how the Christers felt about boys and girls mixing—asked for two separate rooms. They wound up with a spacious sitting room with two connecting bedrooms, each big enough for the whole lot of them to sleep.

Legion flopped down on the huge sofa and kicked off his shoes. "I'm starved. Let's call room service."

"Not." Fade stood over him, hands on hips. "Too much to do. Snack on way out."

Mimic, having reverted to his normal form, dropped down next to Legion. "Out where?"

"Need to get Big Boy and other Legion out of detention camp. And make plans for Hunt day. Tammy, how we find ye friend who know so much about Hunt? Jean, Jane, Joan...?"

"Jeanne Dark," Tammy supplied. "I don't have any idea how to find her. If she's even still alive." Under Fade's relentless stare, Tammy finally said, "I guess we could ask around in the kids' quarter. Someone might know where she is."

"Good," Fade said. "Ye come with me. Legion, split—one with us, other team with Mimic."

"Now I'll be twice as hungry." Nevertheless, Legion divided into two. As long as Colossus and his other self were in the detention camp, he wouldn't rest. He watched his other self stand, then looked at Mimic and sighed. "I suppose I can guess what we're supposed to do?"

Fade nodded. "Spring Colossus and Legion. Bring back here."

"How?"

"Improvise." Fade took the other Legion and Tammy by the shoulders. "March, kiddos."

"All right," Legion called after her, "but tonight I want the biggest dinner you've ever seen. Followed by a good night's sleep."

"Bring back boys," she said over her shoulder, "and Fade will personally feed ye first bite." She threw him a wink. "All six o' ye."

❖

Legion sat on his bunk, both feet flat on the floor, squirming now and again to find a more comfortable position on the hard mattress. After the long train ride, he was sick and tired of sitting, but he didn't dare lay down. He'd tried that, and the counselor's switch left a centimeter-wide welt across his left bicep.

A meter away, Colossus sat, similarly squirming but welt-free. A meter in the other direction, another boy, and another, and another. All told, there were twenty boys in this bunkhouse, and every one of them sat stiffly, watching the counselor pace back and forth between them, listening to his droning voice, waiting for the whistle of the switch.

"You're not bad boys," the counselor was saying. "I don't believe that the good Lord made any truly bad boys. You just need discipline. That's why your parents sent you here, to get a taste of the discipline that made this country great."

That was the fiction—that each and every boy here had been sent by concerned and loving parents. Legion already knew, from whispered conversations in the bathroom and during exercise period, that the parents of most of these boys had thrown them out, abandoned them, or worse.

The only bad thing about these boys was their luck... runaways, they'd had the bad luck to get caught. Caught, and sent to this charming camp that the boys called Reform School.

Four hours here, and already Legion was heartily sick of it.

The counselor had given him and Colossus ill-fitting jumpsuits and work boots, assigned them bunks, and then started on the hard but rewarding work of disciplining them. But he had missed their earplants, and whenever he was able Legion mumbled to his friends, describing the camp's layout and taking what comfort he could from their concern.

"May the Lord bless and keep you," the counselor said. "All right, it's lights out. You'll be up with the sun tomorrow." He looked directly at Legion and Colossus, the new kids. "I'll be in the next room, and I'm a very light sleeper. Stay in your bunks except to use the facilities. The doors are locked and alarmed, so don't even bother trying them." He exited, and the lights cycled down to almost pitch black.

Legion stretched out on the bunk, grateful for any position other than sitting. For the moment, it felt good just to move his aching muscles.

He felt movement next to him, heard Colossus whisper, "Can you believe that guy? What was he going on about, anyway?"

"I don't know," Legion whispered back. "I wasn't listening."

"It's dark."

"I know." He listened to the rustle of shifting bodies, Colossus's ragged breathing next to him. Then he put out a hand, touched Colossus on the shoulder. "Gery, you okay?"

The shoulder beneath his hand quaked, and Legion was sure he heard the ghost of a sob. "I-I'm scared."

"Me too."

"What if they can't get us out?"

"Shhh." In the dark, Legion was sure he heard other boys crying. "They will."

"What if they *don't*?"

He tightened his grip. "Then I guess we'll have to get ourselves out. How hard can it be?"

"Right." Colossus sniffed, then said, "D-Do you mind if we...just talk for a while? I couldn't go to sleep."

Legion was dead tired, but he shrugged. "Sure. But get up off the floor. Lay down here."

Colossus crawled onto Legion's bunk, then snorted. "Oh, I just bet the Christers are going to love *this*." He chuckled. "What do you think our high-and-mighty counselor would do if he saw the two of us in bed with one another?"

"With any luck, die of apoplexy." Legion had plenty of gay friends...in the society of the Myriad Worlds, it was nada problem. Love is love, that's all. And with nonhuman aliens, like Mimic, how could you tell anyway? Besides, it was something every boy tried, now and again...especially a boy who could become identical twins anytime he wanted. But he knew that the Christers had a real problem with it, even worse than they had with boys and girls together.

The Christers, come to think of it, seemed to have a real problem with most things.

He listened to Colossus, saying "uh-huh" every once in a while to show he was paying attention, until the other boy's words faded into nonsense, and Legion drifted away into confused, but happy, dreams.

❖

"Wake up."

"Go away, I'm sleepin'."

"Legion must wake up. Mimic is here to rescue him."

Legion shot upright in his bunk. In the darkness, he could make out Mimic's shape standing above him. "How did you get—?" Stupid question to ask someone who could turn into a fly or a termite or an amoeba. "What's going on?"

"Mimic told you, you are being rescued. Help me wake Colossus; he is deeply asleep."

Colossus was snoring in his own bunk, mouth open and limbs askew, oblivious to the world around him. Legion scrambled to his feet and nudged Colossus, then shook him. The other boy sprang awake with a choked cry. "What?!"

"Get dressed." Legion was pulling on his own coveralls as he spoke. To Mimic, he said, "How are we getting out of here?"

Mimic pointed upward. Four meters above, in the tangle of air ducts and light fixtures than hung just below the ceiling, there was a square that showed stars. "Mimic found a hatch. It was locked, so Mimic made himself a key."

"How do we get up there?"

Stupid question. Colossus stood in the aisle and, silently, enlarged until his head was right below the hatch. He reached down and lifted Legion, then Mimic. Finally, he took hold of the hatch and shrunk to his normal size. Legion and Mimic helped him crawl up to the peaked roof.

Legion's other self was waiting there for him. The two boys faced one another, joined hands, and melted together.

There were the usual moments of confusion, like a dream that lingered in the first seconds after awakening, as nearly two days worth of memories blurred and fused. Legion stumbled, caught himself, then looked around, taking deep breaths fresh air smelling of pine. The sky was clear, with a bright gibbous moon; a sky spattered with stars and endlessly deep. Beneath him the corrugated metal roof still held the day's warmth. Nearby, other similar buildings stood, and a few hundred meters away the camp's high fence cut a geometrical line through the night.

Colossus said, "Great. How do we get away from here? That fence is covered with motion-sensors, and I noticed infrared security beamers all around the compound."

Legion wondered the same thing—and, simultaneously, knew the answer. He put a hand on Mimic's shoulder, flesh cool and leathery beneath his fingers. "Can you handle it? Once more, then we can all rest."

"Mimic can do it." He took a deep breath, then his body started to shift like the moonshadows of trees that danced below them in a gentle wind. Like a butterfly emerging from its chrysalis, Mimic's body unfolded, then unfolded again, stretching....

Scales developed, claws, teeth...then, the transformation apparently complete, Mimic stood before them as a sinuous, four-meter snakelike creature with multifaceted eyes above an alligator snout. He stretched, and great wings unfolded like the sails of an ancient oceangoing vessel.

Picking his way carefully, Legion mounted the beast just above its mighty shoulders, then offered his hand to Colossus. The other boy whistled. "I didn't know he could do *that*."

"He said that a dragon was the only flying form he knew that could carry passengers."

Scrambling onto Mimic's back, Colossus said, "But... dragons are mythical beings."

The great wings beat, and together the three PsiScouts rose into the night air, a hundred meters nearly straight up; then Mimic turned, and they glided off to the east.

"Apparently," Legion said, "not on *his* planet."

❖

All day and into the night, Fade sought Tammy's friend Jeanne.

From one abandoned building to another, they worked their way through the sections of Denver that kids had claimed for their own. To Fade and Legion, the social pattern was familiar; although the kids called their groups "families" instead of "gangs," they would have been comfortable anywhere in Earth's ganger subculture. A family consisted of anywhere from half a dozen to a hundred teeners, all owing allegiance to one leader. There were enough empty buildings that each family had at least one of their own.

Fade gathered that gang rivalry was as important to Denver's teener families as to the New York gangs she knew...but since the Easter hunt, she learned, there had been a general truce. The teeners, united against their common enemy, had closed ranks and were helping one another.

Most of Tammy's erstwhile family died in the hunt, but she knew enough kids from other families to secure safe passage for the PsiScouts. Fade, Legion, and Tammy moved systematically through the city, talking to one leader after another. Fade did most of the talking, with Legion and Tammy to interpret when necessary. Each time, the spiel was roughly the same: she asked after Jeanne Dark and about the details of the hunt; she demonstrated her own psi ability and had Legion demonstrate his; and she asked for the kids' support in bringing an end to the hunt.

Results were disappointing. Everyone knew Jeanne Dark; some had not seen her for weeks, others had talked to her the day before. As for ending the hunt, most of them agreed that it would be wonderful, and that they would cooperate...but none really believed it possible.

Night fell, and still they were no closer to finding Jeanne. As they walked along the dark, deserted street, Fade said in exasperation, "Tammy, ye sure she for real?"

Tammy didn't answer.

"I think we've talked to every gang in this city," Legion said. "And I haven't had anything to eat since lunch. I'm cold and I'm hungry and I'm bored."

"What else be new, kiddo?" She sighed. "All right, we call it a day. Head home, chilluns. Try again tomorrow."

The hotel was about a mile away; halfway there, Fade's communit signaled and she answered it. She listened, then turned to Tammy and Legion with a smile. "Legion and Colossus free. On their way back to hotel with Mimic. Should be there by the time we are."

"Come on," Legion said, racing ahead. "What are you waiting for?"

❖

Mimic, as Reverend Koroli, told Room Service that he had five hungry teenagers to feed and price was no object; this resulted in three trays laden with a smorgasbord of hot and cold dishes that was extensive enough to make even Legion admit he'd had enough. Colossus begged for champagne; Fade allowed one bottle, which all shared. The Scouts gathered in the living room, alternately telling their stories of what they'd done that day, amid much kidding and laughter.

When all the stories were told and the trays had been reduced to leftovers, and the kids were just beginning to feel the impact of the busy day they'd had, there was a knock on the door. "Housekeeping."

"I'll get it." Colossus bounded to the door and swung it open. A stooped, brown woman shuffled in, carrying a double armload of white-slipped feather pillows. Colossus shut the door, and the woman crossed the room, dropped the pillows on the couch, and straightened up. She was still only a little taller than Legion.

She cleared her throat. "I understand you've been looking for me?"

Fade frowned. "Got enough pillows, thanks."

The woman met her eye. "I am Jeanne Dark. I understand that you've been looking for me."

"Jump back," Fade said. "Jeanne Dark be teener, not 'dult."

The woman strode over to Fade, glancing at Tammy as she passed. "I went to an awful lot of trouble to get Tammy out of here. What do you think you're doing, bringing her back?"

Fade tossed her head; Legion recognized the beginnings of the intricate ritual by which the leaders of rival gangs established dominance. "Tammy, this look like ye friend Jeanne?"

"No, but..."

The woman (Jeanne?) advanced another step, so that she was almost toe-to-toe with Fade. "Obviously you've never heard of disguises."

"Ain't no disguise, lady. Last time *ye* be teener, be before my momma and poppa met."

"There are disguises, and there are disguises." The woman reached out a hand. "Take it."

Fade clasped the woman's hand. Then the woman shivered, pulled back, shrunk into herself—and Fade turned slowly around, as if taking in the panorama of the room, before taking the woman's hand again.

Once more the woman transformed, standing up straight, facing Fade head on. This time it was Fade who stepped back, steadying herself as she sat on the edge of the bed.

"Tell them," the woman said.

"Sh-she take over my body." Fade looked even paler than usual. "Like I be passenger, see things but no control."

The Housekeeping woman shrugged. "It's what I do. Witchcraft, a gift from God, I don't know. I can enter the body of anyone I touch. Usually they don't remain conscious." She nodded in Fade's direction. "You've got a strong will."

"Ye too," Fade admitted.

"The authorities know what Jeanne Dark looks like, so I can't go running around the city in my own body. I borrowed this poor woman's for the evening."

Colossus stood with his hands on his hips. "And I guess she doesn't mind?"

"She doesn't *know*. She doesn't have a home or a job; she lives in the park and sits on a corner in the financial section all day, begging for loose change. She fell asleep at dusk; when she wakes up, she'll find that she's had a bath, a good meal, and that someone tucked a hundred dollars in her pocket while she was asleep." Again she shrugged. "You tell me if she minds."

"All right, so ye be Jeanne Dark. What ye want?"

"You're the one who wants to see me. Who are you, and what do *you* want?"

Fade nodded. "Fair 'nough. We be PsiScouts. Come from outside." She indicated the others, one at a time. "Colossus. Mimic. Legion. Tammy ye know. And I be Fade." She took a breath. "We come to end the Hunt."

Jeanne laughed. "Just like that, huh? I guess you're going to send a letter to the Council of Bishops asking them to stop it, eh? What do you want me for, to give you their address?" She laughed again. "Tammy, you should've stayed on the outside. Your new friends are crazy."

"Not like that," Fade answered. "We have talents, too. Big Boy, show."

Colossus grew, until he had to crouch down to avoid the ceiling. Then, in turn, Legion multiplied, Mimic morphed into a tawny-furred tiger, and Fade became invisible. When she reappeared, the others reverted to their own forms.

"Well," Fade said, "What ye think?"

"All right," Jeanne said, "I'm impressed. I thought I was the only one who could pull tricks like that."

"No tricks. Real."

"That's what I meant. Do you have a plan?"

"Do we ever. First, need to know how ye fit in."

"I hate the Hunt. Ever since I heard about it, I've been trying to stop it. Every month, I go out with them. I know where all the best paths are, where kids can hide until it's over, the quickest routes to the tunnel." She glanced at Tammy. "You were almost there when they shot you. So I jumped into your body and gave you the strength to get through the tunnel. I hated to leave you out there, but I had to get back to my own body."

"Thought ye had to touch people?"

"Only to enter their bodies. When I want to leave, I just relax, and snap back into my own."

"So ye know the Hunt layout?"

"Like my own bedroom."

"Good."

"So now will you tell me what you're planning?"

Fade grinned. "Sit down, girl...."

❖

Thursday morning, the PsiScouts became members of Jeanne Dark's gang. They left the hotel and moved into the middle floors of what had once been a towering office building. Jeanne's teeners had repaired broken windows, replaced faulty plumbing and broken elevators, even tapped into the city's energy grid for electricity. They'd painted the walls, inside and out, in garish and intricate patterns, and from all around the city they had gathered chairs, beds, tables, curtains, and other furnishings. As soon as the

PsiScouts entered, Legion was aware of a rich aroma composed of old wood, bread baking in a nearby oven, and the million-and-one scents of human beings living together.

Once, it may have been an office building...now, it was a home.

Jeanne met them in her proper body. She was shorter than Legion by at least five centimeters, pale and covered with freckles, and her spiked hair was bright red. Legion liked her as soon as he saw her.

"Welcome to the madhouse," Jeanne said, giving each of them a quick hug. "We cleared out some rooms along the same hallway so you can have a place to work together." She led them to a stairway, then up two floors to a warren of interconnected rooms. "I've got a 3D map of the Hunt site on the terminal, and I've been adding the things I know about." She shrugged. "Unless you want breakfast first...?"

"Maybe eat and work here?"

"Sure. Things are pretty loose around here. We take turns on cook duty, usually leave breakfast stuff set up in the caf until it gets so gross somebody throws it away. Lunch, you take your chances—one day somebody'll be inspired and make a huge meal, other days everybody scrounges in the kitchen. Dinner goes out about six, seven, or when anybody's hungry enough." Jeanne grinned. "We tend to eat in shifts a lot. I doubt there's ever a time when everybody's together for a meal."

Fade nodded. "Legion, two o' ye help Jeanne carry."

"And bring enough for *everybody*," Colossus called out.

"Rest o' ye, gather round. Bring terminals. Time to plan, chilluns."

Legion split into three. As two of his bodies followed Jeanne, Fade addressed the other PsiScouts. "Okay, who want t' get on Net 'n find Loj-boy?"

Slowly, Legion raised his hand. "That would be me, I guess."

"Good. Let know when ye got 'im."

Just as the C.S.A. was sealed off from the rest of the world by the Curtain of Faith, ChristNet was sealed off from EarthNet. The few contact points were heavily defended against unauthorized intruders. Legion worked on the problem studiously, hardly noticing when his returning selves merged. Sitting before the terminal, lost in its cyberspatial reaches, he gobbled breakfast with one hand, hardly aware of what he ate. Then, tongue protruding from the corner of his mouth and hands typing furiously, he lost all consciousness of time passing.

A hand on his shoulder startled him back to the real world. Colossus stood next to him, frowning. "It's time to take a break, kid. You've been at it for hours."

"I just don't get it," Legion said. "Loj said he was going to be monitoring the Nets for us. I can't believe he'd have any trouble getting into ChristNet. But where is he?"

Colossus pulled up a chair and sat down before the terminal. "Let's see...what've you done so far?"

Legion's fingers flew over the keys. "I've located every gateway between ChristNet and EarthNet. There are thirty-six. Each one is wrapped up in tight security. I've tried all the standard picks and ferrets and moles, and I just can't get through."

"Hmmm. Maybe you're just not thinking like Loj."

"Praise the Lord." Legion frowned. "What do you mean?"

"Here, get a netsearch prompt. We assume that Loj is like us...if he wants to get into ChristNet, he'll work through EarthNet. But maybe that's not how he sees it at all."

"Of course. He's linked to Aarnal. Instead of working through EarthNet, he'll be using whatever they have for a Net. What should I do?"

"Query for references to Aarnal. No, that's too many. Narrow by category."

"I'll try 'network.'"

"Nothing. Try excluding categories. Remove all sermons... now take out general articles, news, that kind of thing."

After excluding every category they could think of, there were still thousands of references. "We can't look through all of those."

"Wait," Colossus said. "Restore the original search. Now narrow by keyword."

"What term should I type in?"

Colossus smiled. "PsiScouts."

In another second, the display blossomed with a single text message: a ChristNet netcode where they could reach BioLogic 17.

"Fade," Legion called, "We've got Loj. Do you want to talk to him now?"

"Ye done good, kiddos. Yeah, bring Brainy Boy up. We talk."

When BioLogic 17 appeared on the screen, he seemed unsurprised to see them. "I was beginning to wonder if you had converted," he said.

"Gods forbid," Fade answered. "Loj, we need ye do some things for us."

He bowed his head. "Your wish is my command, oh leader."

Fade ticked off on her fingers: "Number one, shut up. Number two, need t' talk to Jav-man. He there?"

"Jav is currently conducting an interview with the ambassador from the planet Gh'Rhedd. I can contact him shortly, then you may talk to your heart's content."

"Fine. Number three, need hardware. Two, three, more remote pickups, audividi."

BioLogic sighed. "You don't ask for much, do you? I do not think I can arrange deliveries of materiel into the C.S.A."

"Wasn't askin' ye to. Must be somethin' here we can use. Smart boy like ye, be able t' figure it out."

Frowning, BioLogic answered, "There are audiovisual pickups in your communits. I can instruct one of you how to unship them and mount them on any handheld piece of equipment. The result will not be of the highest quality, but certainly better than the antiquated terminal you're now using."

"Good. Legion, Colossus, ye do what Brainy Boy says. But first number four, an' it's a biggie."

"I am ready."

"Want ye t' take over broadcast links on ChristNet, so we can send our own signal."

"Let me make sure I understand. You want me to usurp control of the live datafeed of a nationwide network—bypassing all security routines and local control—and substitute your data for scheduled programming?"

"Spot on, kiddo."

"Processing." His eyes grew vacant. Legion counted ten, fifteen seconds...then BioLogic returned to himself. For just a moment, Legion wondered how many of Aarnal's linked minds had been working on their little problem. "I believe we can compose and deliver a virus that will do the necessary reprogramming. I am not confident that we can retain control of the network for more than 2048 seconds under the best conditions."

"Half hour. Perfect. Probably need less. Can ye have it ready Sunday?"

"I think so."

"Good." Fade turned away from the screen and addressed the others. "We be on our way. Operation Miracle starts Sunday dawn."

Legion wished he felt as confident as she sounded....

❖

For the next two days, the PsiScouts rested. Legion thought it was a good idea; he knew that he was feeling ragged after so many splits in so little time, and he could only imagine how worn-out Mimic must be. Fade and Jeanne talked to Loj and Jav, ensuring that all their plans were coordinated.

On Friday afternoon, with plenty of warning among the gangs, the police moved through the kids' quarter. As Tammy had said, the cops didn't seem to be trying very hard; they cruised through the streets and nabbed any kid they spotted, but didn't take the trouble to enter any buildings. Jeanne, watching, shook her head. "They don't anticipate any problem reaching their quota. My spies say that there are only about eight hundred hunters in town. This is going to be a small one."

"Eight hundred dead teeners still way too many," Fade answered.

On Saturday afternoon, Fade assembled the PsiScouts in the office that had become their workroom. Tammy and Jeanne were also present.

"Come dark," Fade said, "cops put hunt zone behind curtain. Can't get in, can't get out. We leave now, make it in plenty time. Need to split up. Tammy with Legion, Colossus with Mimic, Jeanne with me. Stay in touch. Meet at main gate to compound, 2100. Lots to do tonight, kiddos. Ever'body okay?"

"We all know the plan," Colossus said. "We've been over it a million times. Let's *go!*"

"One last. We take big chance here. What PsiScouts do. Tammy, Jeanne be volunteers, eyes open, know what they get into. Other teeners, caught by cops or sent to Camp—they don' volunteer." She narrowed her eyes and looked from one to the other as if searching their souls. "We here to stop hunt forever, that be top priority. But we also here to keep teeners safe. Choice between one o' them and one o' us...well, you know who lose."

"It shouldn't come to that," Jeanne said. "Not if we follow the plan exactly."

"Good. All right, Scouts, let's go!"

❖

Legion shivered, glad of the borrowed sweater that Jeanne had insisted he bring. It had been a long and very busy night, but now the sky was growing lighter and there was a hint of red in the east. He yawned and stretched, rubbing his eyes. He knew he should be tired, but he wasn't—not even a little. Instead, he felt exhilarated, keyed up, a bit nervous.

Any moment now, according to Jeanne, the Hunt's directors would open a gate in the curtain and start preparing for the day's activities. Trucks would come in with food and drink for the hunters; weapons dealers for those who wanted to upgrade the power of their killingry; officials to certify each kill; ministers to bless the proceedings; specialists to clean and mount the trophies; specialists of quite another kind to prepare and serve the meat, which after all couldn't be taken home from the hunting grounds—

It was at that point, that Legion had stopped listening to Jeanne's predictions.

Today, that would all come to an end.

Within the fence, over eight hundred teeners and kiddos— some as young as nine or ten—had been told what to do. Five of Legion's doubles, along with Tammy and Mimic, were among the kids to help keep order. Jeanne, Fade, Colossus, and Legion number six now waited outside, concealed in the trees about a hundred meters from the campsite. They could see the main gate, but were themselves invisible.

"I hope this works," Colossus whispered to Legion. "I'm going to be sore for a week, what with all that pushing." Jeanne had shown them a firebreak, a twenty-meter-wide strip of cleared land that ran arrow-straight across the mountains to within half a kilometer of the Red Hill Pass tunnel. During the night, Colossus had shoved trees aside to make a path from firebreak to tunnel, and another from the near end of the firebreak to only a hundred meters from the camp.

"It'll work," Legion answered. "Fade and Jeanne know what they're doing." Legion, like his counterparts, was carrying a makeshift audividi pickup; he tapped the contact button and said softly, "Jav, you there?"

"Ready and waiting," Jav responded, his voice uncharacteristically subdued. "The vidfeed is coming through fine. We're going to have quite a show, my friends."

"Shhh," Jeanne hissed, pointing.

The silvery-grey surface of the Curtain was beginning to unravel in one area; in a matter of seconds, a semicircle had opened in the field, and vehicles began entering in a long, single-file procession.

Jeanne gripped Fade's arm. "Look. In that car. It's the Western Supreme Bishop."

"Big man, nyet? Like Earth President?"

"Only the most powerful man in the country."

"*Western* Bishop...ye got more than one?"

"Eastern and Western. The two voices of God. Except they hate one another."

"Eastern guy, he be watching our show?"

"He won't be able to avoid it, if your friend on the outside knows what he's doing."

"Good. We give 'im *great* show."

❖

At precisely the stroke of eight o'clock, Supreme Bishop Higgs fired a shot into the air, signaling the opening of the Hunt. The gates to the children's compound flew open, and a black mass of frightened teeners and kiddos started to move forward.

At eight o'clock Sunday morning—ten o'clock in the populous eastern cities—tens of millions of Christians were in church, or at home in front of their vidscreens, waiting for the weekly installment of *The Angel Hour*, the highest-rated network broadcast in the country. Jeanne and Tammy had assured the PsiScouts that nine out of ten Christers, in church or out, would be watching.

"This be it, kiddos. Hit it, Jav."

Across the Christian States...and through the Myriad Worlds, wherever subscribers were turned to Jav's program... the opening bars of *The Angel Hour* theme were interrupted by a triple tone, and Jav appeared on the screen. He was dressed in neutral grey, his hair was short and he'd taken off all his personal jewelry. He looked the very epitome of the Christer news announcer.

"Ladies and gentlemen, my brothers and sisters in the Lord, we take you to a site just outside Denver, Colorado in the Christian States of America on Earth...where a shocking scandal has come to our attention."

"Yer cue, Big Boy," Fade called.

Legion lifted his audividi pickup and stepped away from the trees, so he had a good angle on the camp. The device bore two tiny vidscreens; one showed what the machine saw, the other displayed the live feed of Jav's program. In his ear, Jav's editron whispered, "Legion Six, keep close on the Supreme Bishop. We will be cutting to his reaction throughout the program."

The camp came into view, the confused and frightened faces of the teeners, the waiting Hunters holding their guns, the slightly puzzled, froglike smile of the Supreme Bishop. Jav, calmly and evenly, continued. "This is the scene from Pike Forest, where we have learned that hundreds of children have been held overnight. These children have just been released...but they are not free to go. In fact, to Bishop Higgs and nearly a thousand others, they are no longer children—they have become prey."

Tight close-up on a projectile rifle cradled in camouflage-clothed arms.

The teeners, following orders despite their obvious fear, stayed put just inside the gate.

"For over a year, helpless children like these have been sent, or found their way, to Denver. Once a month they are rounded up like stray dogs, then dropped in this forest to become sport for the lucky men who buy a space in the National Hunt."

Quick montage of images from commercials for the Hunt.

"It seems that today, a higher power has taken an interest in the Hunt."

Fade stepped forward, intangible, moving through trees and underbrush. A trick of the light—along with Jav's special effects—made her seem to glow with a cool, white light. She stopped about five meters from the Supreme Bishop, who was frantically conferring with an aide.

"Bishop Higgs," Fade said, and her voice filled the clearing. "I am a messenger from the Lord. He is displeased with what He sees here."

"Young lady," the Bishop drawled, "you don't know what you're interferin' with here."

"The Lord God sees all."

"Ah will not have you blasphemin' in front of me." He jerked his head in her direction. "Get her."

Two black-clothed men—Higgs' bodyguards?—attempted to tackle Fade. She stood still, serene, while their arms went right through her. After a few tries they backed off, confused.

"Oh, for Christ's sake," the Bishop muttered. He lifted his rifle, aimed at Fade's heart, and fired.

The shot passed right through her body, and suddenly the clearing was quiet. Bishop Higgs paled.

Fade lifted one arms, pointing at the trees from which she'd come. "As the Lord promised, let the innocent children come to him."

Now it was Colossus' turn. Soaring twenty-five meters above the crowd, he pushed aside the last of the trees between the camp and his path to safety. Then, ripping the chain-link fence from the soil, he bent it around the Bishop and the waiting Hunters, penning them against the curtain and its opening to the outside.

The teeners surged forward, a mob with some semblance of order, along the path to freedom.

Fade moved toward the Bishop, one relentless step after another, her face still blank but her eyes fixed on Higgs'. It was a wonder, Legion thought, that the man was able to function at all.

"The Lord calls upon the Eastern Bishop, and upon all the citizens who hear His word, to bring an end to this shameful travesty. Let the tradition of the Hunt end today."

Higgs stood up straight at the twisted fence, towering over Fade. He was a bulky man, boarlike, and he dwarfed the PsiScout. "Now you listen to me, little lady. A few virtie special effects don't convince me that you're the messenger of the Lord. These men," he waved at the Hunters, "have worked hard and paid a lot of money for the privilege of participating in this event, and ah do not intend to disappoint them. Everything we do here is the will of the Lord."

"You are a liar and a blasphemer."

Jeanne, Tammy, and several other Legions were gathered around now, directing the throng of kids on their way.

"Ah don't know what you've been told is happening here —"

"Innocent children are being hunted down and killed like game animals."

"There you are seriously mistaken." Higgs caught sight of Legion's pickup, and turned to face it with the poise of an accomplished televangelist. "The Lord has made it possible for children from poor families, from the cities, to come out here and enjoy a day in the wilderness. A chance for these children...runaways, orphans, those with no father figures at home...to spend some time with adults, selfless men who volunteer their time as big brothers to these children—and here you are trying to shut the whole program down with a few cheap effects and some flashy camera techniques?" He was warming to his subject. "It's the power of the Devil, child, that makes you say and do these things. Come close and let me give you the blessing of the Lord...."

Incredibly, the kids themselves had stopped to listen. Legion felt the whole plan slipping away. What good did it do, for everyone in the C.S.A. to see this, if Higgs could weasel things around like this?

Tammy pushed forward, opening her blouse to show her scars. "*This* is how your big brothers are treating us. I was close to dead! This is no vacation in the woods—it's a massacre." She lifted her audividi pickup. "I want the whole *world* to see what you're doing here." She aimed the pickup at Higgs.

Out of the corner of his eye, Legion saw one of the bodyguards lift a small pistol. Before he could cry out a warning, the weapon discharged silently. Tammy stumbled backward, then fell to the ground, her white blouse splattered with crimson.

Colossus swatted the bodyguards, sending them tumbling into the curtain's field. Fade rushed to Tammy, knelt by her, and solidified to lift the girl's limp body.

It was Jeanne, though, whom Legion watched. Eyes aflame, the girl sprinted to the fence, climbed over it in a single motion, and dropped on Higgs. There was a momentary struggle, then the Bishop rose, Jeanne crumpled and still at his feet.

He turned to the other 'dults. "Stop! Leave here! The Hunt is cancelled. I will commune with these messengers from the Lord." Of course. Jeanne had used her psi ability, had possessed him and was speaking through his mouth.

The 'dults were not fooled. Helpers and hunters both moved closer, like a noose tightening around the PsiScouts. The plan had gone all to pieces, and Legion couldn't think of what to do.

Fade rose to her feet, Tammy's limp body on the ground before her. Her face was wet with tears as she faced the hunters; Legion brought up his audividi and zoomed in. "Hope ye're happy," she shouted. "Ye killed her. Ye hunters, ye Christers, ye people watching in Myriad Worlds—ye *all* killed her. Kids be slaughtered, an' ye all sit by and watch." Fade spat. "Hope ye happy, is all I can say."

Higgs stumbled back, and Jeanne stood up. Again she was over the fence in an instant, pushing through Fade's intangible body, kneeling by Tammy. Jeanne embraced the prone girl, and there was a momentary flash that hurt Legion's eyes. He blinked, and suddenly Tammy was alive, Jeanne motionless before her.

Tammy struggled to her feet, her face and hands pale against her crimson-spattered dress. She looked up to the sky, and an errant sunbeam (or was it one of Jav's special effects?) lit her visage. The crowd, teeners and hunters alike, grew quiet as Tammy said to the sky, "Lord God of Hosts, all power and glory is Thine." She lowered her gaze to the hunters. "Hear the word of the Lord. These are My beloved children; whoso harms a hair on their heads harms Me, and he shall suffer My wrath through eternity. My vengeance shall be upon him and his house."

Higgs dropped to his knees, followed by the assembled hunters. "Lord," he shouted, "I have felt Your touch, and I repent. Merciful Lord, spare us, Your humble servants."

Tammy took a few steps forward, looking down on Higgs. In a softer tone, she said, "The Lord your God commands you to leave this place, Gerald Higgs, you and all your fellows. Return not. The Hunt, which is an abomination in the sight of the Lord, shall never be again. So the Lord God commands."

"Thank you, oh Lord."

"The children shall pass in peace, and they will find comfort in the kingdom of Heaven."

"Yes, Lord."

"Know then, says the Lord, that these are His angels, and they shall pass invisibly among you, so that He will know if you break His commands. Mark them well and honor them, for they are the faithful servants of the Lord." Tammy took a ragged breath, then pointed at the gate. "Go, now, and never return to this place."

Legion watched, amazed, as the hunters stood, brushed themselves off, and retreated through the exit. Bishop Higgs was the last to go, bowing and scraping all the way. Then the exit dilated, and the curtain was sealed once more.

Legion ran to support a faltering Tammy. "You were great! We thought for sure that...that you were...."

"Get...trucks. Need to get kids...to the tunnel...to safety."

"You're weak." She'd lost a lot of blood. "What about Jeanne?"

"I...am...Jeanne." With that, she fainted, and it was all Legion could do to keep her from falling to the ground.

❖

It was a harrowing ride to the tunnel; Legion expected the Army of God to show up in force at any moment. Only when the tunnel and the Curtain of Faith were behind them, and he saw Earth Police ships descending, did he finally relax. Med techs took Jeanne and Tammy at once, while other EP's lifted refugee teeners from the trucks.

It was cold and they were tired, but the PsiScouts stayed until all of the other teeners were loaded aboard transports, to begin new lives in the Myriad Worlds. Zhene Carmody and De' Taurid were on the last ship; they draped the Scouts with blankets and gave them hot tea, and listened to their story.

"I don't get it," Colossus said. "Why'd they give up at the end? They had us."

De' Taurid replied, "Seeing Tammy rise from the dead was what did it. You'd done an excellent job of pushing all their buttons...angelic visitors, God's wrath, and all of it on nationwide video. The populace was on your side right away, but Higgs and the others didn't know they were on video. Still, when Tammy sat up, that was it. They couldn't doubt any longer."

"What with her?" Fade asked. "First she dead, then it's hello, Angel of the Lord. How she do that?"

De' Taurid and Zhene exchanged glances. "You don't know?" Zhene said.

"Don' know what?"

"Tammy *was* dead. Clinically, psychologically. Jeanne took over her body."

Legion felt a shiver. "I didn't know she could do that."

"She didn't, either. It was a terrible shock to her system. She's in psych-treatment now. As near as the techs have managed to piece together, the shock fused Jeanne's personality with the remnants of Tammy's memory-traces. It's going to take some very careful treatment for her to recover."

"Wait, what ye sayin'? Jeanne took over Tammy's body, but we saved both. Jeanne can come back to own body now, nyet?"

"Fade, the shock of fusion stopped Jeanne's heart. Her body was too far gone for the medtechs to save it." Zhene shook her head. "The girl who's left has Tammy's body, but her mind is a mixture of Jeanne's personality and some of Tammy's memories. Tammy as you knew her is gone."

De' Taurid, weeping, turned away.

"We have to see her," Colossus said.

Zhene nodded. "I anticipated you. We're on the way to the mediplex now."

❖

Jeanne dreams. In her dream, she remembers Tammy. Remembers the sun on Tammy's golden hair, the emerald twinkle in Tammy's eye. Remembers Tammy's home, a modest neo-Colonial with white trim, a rustic wooden fence, and a buttercream collie playing in the yard. Remembers Tammy's school, the teachers she'd loved and the friends she'd made. Remembers Tammy's flight from stifling conventionality, her first glimpse of sprawling, bewildering

Denver, her confusion at all the new sights and tastes and experiences.

Thrashing in her sleep, Jeanne remembers Tammy's first death. Flaming pain and the smell of charred flesh, and then the inner strength that carries her, in spite of herself, to safety in the mountains beyond the Curtain.

Remembers the incoherent wonder of it all: aircars and holoshows and the unfettered freedom of the Net. De' Taurid, with a face like the Holy Mother and a heart to match. The PsiScouts.

The return to Hell.

In Jeanne's dream, Tammy dies again...and again...and again....

Then Jeanne's tossing and turning ends, her gasping breath calms.

Tammy is not dead.

Tammy is here.

She *is* Tammy. She is Jeanne. Both, fused together in one body, one soul.

Jeanne/Tammy, breathing deeply, rests at last in peace.

❖

Jeanne insisted there be no publicity, and in the end Jav agreed. So it was just six of them, on this deserted mountainside, the Curtain of Faith shimmering behind them: Fade, Mimic, Legion, Colossus, De' Taurid, and Jeanne herself.

"She was a sweet girl," De' Taurid said. "She had more courage in her little finger than I have in my whole body. She didn't deserve to die."

"She hasn't died," Jeanne whispered. "She forgives you. She forgives everyone."

"She worked miracles," Colossus said. The C.S.A., according to informers, was in turmoil. Bishop Higgs and his government had resigned; the Hunt was officially abolished;

and there was even talk of the new Western Bishop meeting with delegates from the Myriad Worlds to discuss exit visas for runaway teeners.

"Is time," Fade said, "to move on. Jeanne, we want ye as PsiScout."

"I...I don't know what to say."

"Ye still got ye psi talent, no?"

"I do. But I think it's going to take me a long time to get comfortable with it again."

"Take time ye need. Work wi' psych-techs. Get healthy."

Legion took her hand. "You've got a home with us. Whenever you want, and for however long you want."

De' Taurid looked uneasy. "Of course, if you want to return to your old family, we can arrange it."

Jeanne shook her head. "No." She stood by the Curtain, peering past the shimmering air to the land beyond. "I'm not the girl I was before. I'm neither of them. And I don't think I belong there, any more." She turned to the PsiScouts. "I guess I'll need a new name."

"How about 'Merge?'" Mimic asked.

She considered it for a moment, then smiled. "Yes, I think that'll do. I think I'd like that very much."

"Then come on," Colossus said, turning toward De' Taurid's waiting aircar.

"Wait. One more thing." Merge held out a small canister, marked with official symbols and numbers—all that was left of the body that had been Jeanne Dark's. She opened the canister, and tossed its contents toward the Curtain.

As they struck, the particles sparkled, then settled to the ground on either side of the shimmering force field.

"There," Merge said. "That's the end of that."

She took the arms of her new friends, and together they walked to the car.

❖

Appendix:
The PsiScouts

BioLogic 17 (Ramu Fornix of Aarnal): Age 15. BioLogic 17 is a living computer who can link his mind to the massed computer minds of the planet Aarnal.

Bolt (Gael Rimma of Wargal): Age 15. Bolt's psi powers give her limited control of electrical fields, plus the ability to generate spontaneous electrical currents.

Colossus (Gery Allin of Earth): Age 16. Colossus is able to increase his size and strength at will.

Coulomb (Royd Kar of Taarla): Age 14. Coulomb is a telekinetic with the ability to manipulate the magnetic fields and forces around him.

Do-San (Ut Napis of Ixtal): Age 17. Do-San is virtually invulnerable, and has great strength along with the abilities of flight, clairvoyant senses, and pyrokinesis. He is an honorary member of the PsiScouts.

Fade (Tovi Witzell of Tyzgab): Age 14. Fade can render herself partially or completely invisible and intangible.

Legion (Lethim Barog of Garagk): Age 13. Legion can manifest up to six simultaneous astral bodies, each as apparently solid as his own.

Mentaxa (Iris Krall of Ceres): Age 15. Mentaxa is a powerful and accomplished telepath.

Merge (Jeanne Dark of Earth): Age 16. Merge is able to project her own personality into the body of another; if the other's will is not too strong, she can control the body as if it were hers.

Mimic (Kheen Kharrn of Nortlin): Age 14. Mimic is a shapeshifter, able to take on the shape of any object or creature.

Power Lad (Ran-Arl of Ketrus): Age 15. Power Lad, one of the 20th Century's greatest Champions, has numerous psi abilities including flight, clairvoyant senses, pyrokinesis, great strength, and near-invulnerability. As an adult, he is the legendary Champion Power Man. He is an honorary member of the PsiScouts.

Power Maid (Zun-Kela of Ketrus): Age 14. Power Maid shares the psionic abilities of her father, Power Man. She is an honorary member of the PsiScouts.

The Scattered Worlds Mosaic by Don Sakers

Dance for the Ivory Madonna
a romance of psiberspace
Print & Kindle
Spectrum Award finalist; 56 Hugo nominations
"Imagine a Stand on Zanzibar written by a left-wing Robert Heinlein, and infused with the most exciting possibilities of the new cyber-technology." -Melissa Scott,
author of Dreaming Metal, The Jazz

Weaving the Web of Days
a tale of the Scattered Worlds
Print & Kindle
Maj Thovold has led the Galaxy for three decades, a Golden Age of peace and prosperity. She is weary and ready to resign, but she faces one last battle: a battle on the strangest battlefield known: a web of living tendrils that stretches across interstellar space. A web where Maj's enemies wait, like spiders, for their prey....

The Eighth Succession
a novel of the Scattered Worlds
Print & Kindle
"Remember when science fiction used to be filled with galactic intrigue and bigger-than-life heroes? The wonderful Don Sakers certainly does! The Eighth Succession is a rip-roaring yarn, impossible to put down. If John W. Campbell's Astounding Stories had been published in an LGBT-friendly era, this is the cover-story serial you'd have been waiting anxiously for each month. What a ride!" -Robert J. Sawyer, Hugo Award-winning author of Red Planet Blues

Children of the Eighth Day
a novel of the Scattered Worlds
Print & Kindle
The Eighth Succession *introduced readers to the Hoister Family...* Children of the Eighth Day *takes the story of this remarkable family to the exciting next level.*

The Scattered Worlds Mosaic by Don Sakers

All Roads Lead to Terra

two tales of the Scattered Worlds

Kindle only

Two exciting tales tell of attacks against the shining jewel of the Terran Empire: Earth. Includes an introduction and notes from the author.

A Voice in Every Wind

two tales of the Scattered Worlds

Print & Kindle

On a world where meaning lives in every rock and stream, and every breeze brings a new voice, one human explorer stands on the threshold of discoveries that could alter the future of Humanity.

A Rose From Old Terra

a novel of the Scattered Worlds

Print & Kindle

Jedrek left the Grand Library and his work circle eleven years ago. Now a crisis in uncharted space brings the circle back together. Soon, Jedrek and his friends are at the focal point of a clash of cultures, and the only thing that can save the Galaxy is one modest group of Librarians.

The Leaves of October

a novel of the Scattered Worlds

Print & Kindle

Compton Crook Award finalist

The Hlutr: Immensely old, terribly wise…and utterly alien. When mankind went out into the stars, he found the Hlutr waiting for him. Waiting to observe, to converse, to help. Waiting to judge…and, if necessary, to destroy.

More Books from Speed-of-C Productions

The Curse of the Zwilling by Don Sakers
Print & Kindle

It's Hogwarts meets Buffy at Patapsco University: a small, cozy liberal arts college like so many others – except for the Department of Comparative Religion, where age-old spells are taught and magic is practiced. When a favorite teacher is found dead under mysterious circumstances, grad student David Galvin finds that a malevolent evil has awakened. And now David, along with four novice undergrads, must defeat this ancient, malignant terror.

The SF Book of Days by Don Sakers
Print only

Drawn from the pages of classic sf literature, here is a science fiction/fantasy event for every day of the year...and for quite a few days that aren't part of the year. From Doc Brown's arrival in Hill Valley (January 1, 1885) to the launch of the Bellerophon *(Sextor 7, 2351), this datebook is truly out of this world.*

PsiScouts #1: At Risk by Don Sakers & Phil Meade
Print & Kindle

In the 26th century, psi-powered teenagers from all over the Myriad Worlds join together as the heroic PsiScouts.

Meat and Machine: queer writings by Don Sakers
Print & Kindle

Don Sakers has been queering sf and fantasy for three decades. Meat and Machine collects 24 short pieces of Don's science fiction, fantasy, nonfiction, and erotics.

Elevenses by Don Sakers
Print & Kindle

Eleven SF and fantasy short stories intended as bite-size snacks.

More Books from Speed-of-C Productions

Gaylaxicon Sampler 2006
Print only
Sample the work of thirteen writers from across the spectrum of gay, lesbian, bisexual, and/or transgender science fiction, fantasy, and/or horror. Includes big names and small, much-published veterans and promising beginners, Lammy and Spectrum Award nominees and winners, past Gaylaxicon Guests of Honor, and fresh new names.

QSpec Sampler 2007
Print only
Originally prepared as a giveaway at Gaylaxicon 2007 in Atlanta, this volume is available at a nominal charge as a sampler of the fine work being done by GLBT writers in SF, fantasy, and horror.

Act Well Your Part by Don Sakers
Print & Kindle
A beloved gay young adult romance, back in print for its adult fans as well as a new generation of teens. At first Keith Graff dislikes his new school. He misses his old friends, and despairs of ever fitting in. Then he joins the school's drama club, and meets the boyishly cute Bran Davenport....

Lucky in Love by Don Sakers
Print & Kindle
A companion novel to Act Well Your Part, Lucky in Love *follows Keith's friend Frank, torn between bad boy Dwight and basketball star Darnell.*

A Cosmos of Many Mansions: Varieties of SF by Don Sakers
Print & Kindle
Based on the first five years of Sakers's popular review column, this volume examines & explains dozens of types of science fiction along with hundreds of reviews.

The Mud of the Place by Susanna J. Sturgis
Print only
"A sensitive, witty, and tightly plotted portrayal of life on Martha's Vineyard that only a true Islander could have written. Nice going, Susanna!" –Cynthia Riggs

www.ingramcontent.com/pod-product-compliance
Lightning Source LLC
Chambersburg PA
CBHW071232170626
46809CB00013BA/2645